Sasha

Shelley Munro

Munro Press

Sasha

Copyright © 2024 by Shelley Munro

Print ISBN: 978-1-99-106369-4
Ebook ISBN: 978-0-9951395-3-4

Editor: Evil Eye Editing
Cover: Kim Killion, The Killion Group, Inc.

Munro Press, New Zealand.

First Munro Press electronic publication November 2020
First Munro Press print publication November 2024

DEDICATION

For Paul, my husband, partner in crime, and fellow adventurer.
Every day is a good day.

Introduction

Out of options. Out of time.

Sasha, The Lionhearted, is the youngest child and only daughter of one of the main Perfume Isle clans. After Sasha rejects every marriage candidate presented to her, her frustrated parents organize a betrothal to Bruceous, The Businessman. He's much older, and yuck! *Worst contender ever.* The notion of living with this bum-pinching, leering dragonman appalls Sasha.

Furious, she leaves to visit her best friend and never arrives. Her routine flight becomes an adventure when she breaks through the protective barrier surrounding the Dragon Isles. Now, she's trapped on the mainland where humans supposedly persecute dragons.

Maxwell Lombardy is drowning under commitment. After his parents' sudden death, he's responsible for his much younger brother. Max's grandparents have started legal proceedings to gain custody of his brother, and his busy job leaves him with limited time. The nanny option isn't working either until he meets the gorgeous and mysterious Sasha.

Sasha needs a job and accommodation, and Max requires a fake fiancée to present to his grandparents and the court. Problems sorted, except for one slight difficulty. Sparks fly between the pair. Maxwell becomes as enamored as his brother, but his sexy fiancée harbors secrets, and when he discovers what they are—let's say they have the potential to blast his house of cards apart with the force of dragon fire.

Author Note

Welcome to Max's and Sasha's romance, the fourth book in the Dragon Isles series. This book stands alone within the series.

Remember, as in the previous books in the series, some of my setting is real and is what you'll find in the area while in other places, I've used artistic license. My story has cliffs, but in reality, the area is much flatter. I have placed trees where there are none, and Lindisfarne Castle is furnished in the Edwardian style as it was during the period Edward Hudson owned it as a holiday home. Bamburgh Castle, which I have visited, perches on a rocky outcrop and has no gardens.

Just go with it, okay? Enjoy the romance, and please forgive me for my writer's imagination because I couldn't find everything I needed in the way of a setting to keep things real.

I hope you enjoy the adventure and soar with the dragons, and please subscribe to my newsletter if you'd like to keep up with my upcoming releases and news.

Shelley

CHAPTER 1

Ultimatum

Sasha, The Lionhearted, stared at her mother in utter shock while panic pounded her chest. Nausea shot through her, and her vision faded in and out. She gripped the chair armrests while her dragon issued a silent roar. Currently in her tattoo form, her dragon scooted up Sasha's body to reposition for a better view. She peeked over Sasha's collar.

"Ooh, the vein at our mother's neck is ticking."

Sasha ignored the private communication from her dragon and bounded from the comfortable chair. "No! You can't make me. I won't marry Bruceous. He's high-handed, and his behavior is outdated. The last time I saw him, he lectured me for speaking before he granted permission. We don't suit, and I refuse to wed him, no matter what you or Father think is best."

Sun streamed into the solar, highlighting the elegant furnishings and the tasteful pieces of art adorning the walls. Sasha stared at a seascape depicting rocky cliffs and white-crested waves. The sea always calmed her, but the urge to shriek and stomp her feet in a tantrum almost won. Instead, she inhaled and fought for calm. She rounded a straightback chair and faced her mother. Unfortunately, she was wearing trews instead of a dress, and she caught her mother's cringe.

Sasha rushed into speech to stave off a lecture. "Mother, this is sudden. You promised I could choose my husband, that I didn't need to go through a betrothal."

Sadness filled her mother's oval face before the emotion retreated, and determination took its place. "Your father and I have discussed the matter. You have rejected every suitable offer, and it is time for you to grow up and accept the responsibility of a husband."

"Bruceous is thirty years older than me," Sasha whispered. "He's the same age as you."

Her mother flinched. "Older," she admitted.

"Blaze won't agree. He'll side with me."

"It's none of your brother's business," her mother said. "Your father and I will undertake the marriage discussion. Bruceous is visiting tomorrow. You will stand at our side and greet him with a polite smile and the perfect manners I taught you. And you will wear a dress."

"No!" her dragon roared, as appalled as Sasha at spending time in the same room, let alone the old dragon touching them. Intimately. *Ugh! "Let's go,"* her dragon prompted. *"Escape this lecture."*

Sasha whirled away and stomped from the salon, the thick, deep brown carpet spoiling her dramatic exit.

"Come back here," her mother snapped, in a no-nonsense tone.

Sasha kept striding, her heart racing while every instinct shouted for her to escape. Once she reached her bedroom, she slammed the door. She stalked to her carved wooden wardrobe and plucked a dress from inside. After folding the silky fabric with care, she placed it inside a bag. She added stockings and a pair of shoes to wear indoors, her favorite perfume, a comb, and her tooth cleaner. At the last moment, she packed a clean pair of trews, a shirt, and a black woolen jacket before pulling the drawstring on the floral embroidered bag. The last thing she wanted was to strew her belongings along the flight path she used to visit her best friend on the other side of Perfume Isle.

"Sasha, come out here. We need to talk about this." Her mother's voice sounded closer. "Your father and I expect you to be with us when Bruceous arrives."

Sasha inhaled, struggling for composure. Tears pricked her eyes, and she willed them away. Dragons were tough. They didn't cry, but oh! This was so unfair.

"Sasha." Annoyance shaded her mother's tone this time.

"I heard you," Sasha said, and pride radiated through her because her voice remained steady and didn't crack. "I'll be here."

"You'll return this evening. If I don't receive your promise, I'll refuse my permission for you to visit Isobel."

Sasha squeezed her eyes shut. The thought of getting personal with Bruceous brought a shudder of revulsion. He'd pinched her bottom at the Samhain celebration several months ago. Not once, but twice. Disgusting old dragon. If Bruceous leered at her mother in the same way, her parent would have second and third thoughts about this marriage.

"Sasha! Answer me." Impatience snapped in her mother, and it sounded as if she stood right outside Sasha's door.

Sasha wilted for long seconds before straightening her spine. "You have my promise. I will return this evening in time for dinner."

"Don't make me regret giving you this freedom. You won't get another chance."

"Yes, Mother," Sasha said, her stomach twisting. Her parents had warned her if she didn't choose, they'd make a decision for her. Although why she had to marry when her older brothers remained free made no sense.

Silence fell, and Sasha held her breath, praying her mother had finished with her lecture. Eventually, her mother's footsteps retreated, and Sasha relaxed. Her parents assured her they wanted her happiness. Huh! Their choice of dragons was abysmal.

Sasha opened her terrace door and slipped from her clothes. She embraced her dragon, letting the shift take her in an explosion of power. She scooped up her bag in one talon and took to the air.

As always, the rush of freedom filled her with joy. Her pulse raced faster with each flap of her wings. When she glided, everything was peaceful.

"We'll lose what independence we have if we accept Bruceous," her dragon said.

"True," Sasha agreed. *"I'm at a loss to understand why our parents wish this match. Could they be short of money? Or is it because Mother settled with Father when she was younger than us? Let's fly for fun instead of traveling straight to Isobel's house. I wish to skim the waves and feel the sea breeze on our face."*

Her dragon banked away from the land and darted over the sea. Today, the waves reflected the sunlight and appeared a stunning jade green. The clouds were a puffy white, and the faint breeze cleared the cobwebs from her mind.

She'd speak with her brothers on her return. Perhaps they'd help her parents understand a lifelong partnership with Bruceous wasn't suitable for her.

"We're skilled with plants and grow amazing flowers," her dragon said, her tone strident. *"They should give us a chance to prove ourselves. Let us start a business and allow us to embrace our*

courageous *designation.*"

An old, well-trodden discussion between her and her parents. Sasha had broached the subject of more independence, and her mother and father rejected every argument she'd offered. The bottom line—female dragons should follow a proven path rather than trespassing into masculine territory. Daughters must accept the directives handed down from parents since they had their child's best interests at heart.

We only want your happiness, Sasha.

Her parents didn't understand she was at her happiest when her hands were digging in the soil, and she laid her eyes on a plot of beautiful flowers. That was true joy, and her success brought a sense of satisfaction. Her dragon was right—if they acquiesced to this marriage with Bruceous, her limited freedom would dissipate like dragon's smoke.

"We should turn back now," she told her dragon.

"Just a little longer before we visit Isobel."

Sasha scowled at the mention of her friend. Isobel had recently become engaged to a dragon from Hissing Isle. He seemed nice enough. Isobel was happy with the arrangement, but she wasn't crazy-mad in love or attracted to her fiancé.

Sasha wanted to know what came later. Her parents informed her love grew in time, and an arranged relationship was practical for both parties. Sasha doubted she'd ever like, let alone love the ogling Bruceous with his wandering hands.

What happened when he tired of her?

Sasha could easily imagine Bruceous pinching bums and embarrassing her at parties. He'd harassed young females for years, and she doubted he'd change. Others would pity her. Once the news spread, they'd sympathize. Then there was the whole sex thing.

Sex with Bruceous. Yuck!

"Stop those nasty thoughts," her dragon implored. *"You're making me nauseous. If you think Bruceous is bad, you wait until his dragon makes an appearance. I bet he's twice as ugly and even more reptilian than the man."*

"We can't let this betrothal go ahead."

"At least it's a betrothal at this stage and not a marriage."

"Huh!" Sasha spat. *"Once the arrangement becomes formal, there is no wriggling away from Bruceous's trap. I still can't understand why Mother and Father consider this a suitable match. No matter how hard I try to place myself in their shoes, the logic of their decision fails me."*

"The air over there is strange," her dragon murmured. *"Oh, look! Pretty rainbows."*

Before Sasha could caution her dragon, a single wing beat took them gliding through the sparkle of colors. Her dragon faltered at the sudden force of dense air. She strained to move her wings, doubling her effort. Without warning, her dragon shot forward and veered downward. They skimmed the waves and stabilized their flight path.

"*Are you all right? What* was *that?*" Sasha asked.

"*I've never encountered anything of the sort before. The air thickened, and it was exhausting to maintain our height.*"

"*There's land over there. Let's rest on the beach,*" Sasha suggested.

Four slow wing beats later, they landed on a strip of sand.

"*Where are we? I don't recognize this area,*" Sasha said.

Her dragon inhaled and exhaled a breath along with several smoke rings. "*I don't recall the landmarks either. It doesn't smell like Perfume Isle. Where are the spices and the beautifully scented flowers? All I can distinguish is the brine of the sea and a dead animal. A hint of smoke. And a layer of something strange. I can't describe it, but it makes me want to sneeze. Do you know what it is?*"

"*No,*" Sasha said.

"*Wait, is that weeping?*"

Sasha listened along with her dragon. "*The crying is coming from over there. Should we investigate?*"

"*Whoever it is sounds so unhappy. Perhaps we can help. Maybe they'll give us directions to return to Perfume Isle.*"

Sasha frowned, caution making her hesitate. "*We should shift and dress in case it is a human. Our dragon scares some humans.*"

"*But we are beautiful. We are a delightful shimmering bronze color with stunning and unusual blue eyes.*" Her dragon fluttered her eyelashes and preened.

Sasha huffed. "*Our appearance won't help us escape Bruceous.*"

"Unfortunately not. We will do as you suggest."

An instant later, Sasha used human hands to unfasten her bag and pull out clothes. Much to the despair of her mother, Sasha had commandeered her older siblings' discarded apparel. She pulled on black trews, a tight undergarment to support her breasts, and a blue shirt. Last, she shoved her feet in sandals.

"Right," she murmured. "Let's do this."

The sobs had them striding up the beach and into the dunes.

"The hour grows late here," her dragon commented. *"We weren't in the air for that long, yet darkness will fall soon."*

"Ah, there," Sasha whispered. "It is a human child."

"His face looks strange. Too big. Wide and flat."

"Yes, but he's so sad. We have to help him." Sasha crouched, not too close to the child in case she scared him. "Hello there," she said and smiled. "What is making you so sad?"

He knuckled the tears from his almond-shaped eyes and stared at her like an intent owl. "Lost."

"What's your name, sweetie?"

"Noel."

Sasha held out her hand in the way she'd noticed humans did when they met someone new. Noel frowned at her hand before touching it with his fingertips. Confusion filled Sasha. She'd watched humans grip another's hand and pump it up and down for two or three beats. Was this a nuance she'd missed?

"Hello, Noel," she said. "My name is Sasha."

"Shasha?"

His mouth didn't form her name correctly, but she didn't mind.

"Would you like me to help you go home?"

He nodded, his gaze strangely penetrating while the tip of his tongue poked between his lips.

"We need to pick up his trail. If we can't find Noel's scent, we might follow his footprints back to his family," her dragon said.

"He's too young to stay out in the dark alone," Sasha murmured. "Noel, if you hold my hand, I'll take you home."

He rubbed his face and hesitated a beat longer before standing and lifting his hand. Sasha curled her fingers around his and inhaled the air. Although confident she had Noel's scent, she still scanned the ground for his footprints.

"His stride is off," her dragon announced.

"Yes." She walked two steps before she felt the drag on her arm. *"He has a slight limp."*

"He's a funny little fellow. So serious. Not a chatterbox."

Sasha slowed her pace to match Noel's. *"A chatterbox would drive us both crazy."*

"What should we do after we find Noel's home?"

"Where are we is the better question. None of the isles have dunes."

Her dragon paused. *"I cannot sense other dragons. We do when we're on Perfume Isle. There are always other dragons around, or at least their scent fills the air. I cannot smell a single one here."*

"We should maintain our human form until we learn our

13

location. Can you sense other humans?"

"No, just Noel."

"Ugh, it appears Noel walked in circles for a long time. No wonder he was upset." Sasha surveyed the scuffed footprints in the sand. The scent trail worked best, although that led them in large circles too. The sun passed beneath the horizon, taking the last of the light. Other than the swish of the waves and a lone bird wheeling across the sky, Sasha could hear nothing.

"Don't like dark," Noel whispered, his small fingers clenching hers tighter. "Can't see."

"You're in luck then," Sasha chirped. "I have excellent night vision. We'll have you home in no time."

Maxwell Lombardy pulled up in front of his childhood home with a tired sigh. The meeting in Edinburgh had been a long, brutal one with heads rolling. He was damn lucky the boss understood his situation and appreciated the work ethic he'd established since joining the newspaper. Max grabbed his laptop bag out of the back along with his suit jacket and started for the house. At least he'd made it home before Noel's bedtime. He'd read his brother a bedtime story. That always relaxed Max, and his brother seemed to enjoy the ritual they'd established.

It took him long seconds to realize the house lay in unnatural darkness, given Sheryl should be preparing dinner or even doing the dishes. Max started running. He burst through the unlocked front door and flicked on the hall light.

"Sheryl? Sheryl! Noel, I'm home."

No one replied, and when his little brother didn't come barreling from the family room to say hello, Max truly started to worry. Sheryl and Noel should be here. The scent of dinner should waft on the air. True, Sheryl often burned the meal when she became involved in her soap operas, but at least Noel appreciated her culinary efforts.

Max set his laptop bag and suit jacket on the kitchen table. Dirty dishes littered the countertop, and an empty crisp packet lay in the middle of the floor, its meager contents spilled across the dirty tiles.

Max continued his search, his pulse racing. He rapidly scanned the mudroom where they stored gumboots and wet-weather gear. The open external door was ominous. Hell, had his grandparents barged into the house and taken Noel without telling him? His grandmother had threatened to do that before, citing his lack of years and feminine influence as a reason his younger brother was at risk under Max's care. Total bull crap. Max loved his brother, who was an enthusiastic and happy child, despite the Down syndrome that many people used to define him.

"Noel?" Max checked the formal dining room, the family room where he and Noel watched TV together, the second lounge where they entertained his grandparents, and the downstairs bathroom before heading upstairs to check the bedrooms. He searched Noel's first. His favorite toys were present. His bedspread bore crinkles as if Noel had taken a nap at some stage during the day.

Noel wasn't present, full of smiles and a welcome for his big brother. Max even searched the closet where Noel hid if something upset him or he was out of sorts. His brother had spent way too many hours in that hidey-hole after their parents had died in the accident. Max had thought—hoped—Noel had started to accept their absence.

It was quiet up here too. Max found his bedroom was empty, as was the bathroom, the separate toilet, and his parents' bedroom. Max had considered moving into the master, but it had upset Noel, so he'd kept using his old room.

Still nothing. Where the devil were they?

Surely if his grandparents had taken Noel, Sheryl would've been here or at least called him to let him know. He considered ringing his grandparents, but if Noel weren't with them, the phone call would start a chain reaction he'd never stop.

He reached Sheryl's bedroom and opened the door. On hearing a muffled sound, he flicked on the light. Sheryl lay on the bed, snoring, and not even the abrupt illumination jerked her awake. Another snore erupted from her, loud enough to rattle the rafters. A bottle of what looked like vodka sat on the bedside cabinet, along with an open bottle of orange juice and an empty glass. Only an inch of the vodka remained.

With two strides, Max reached the bed and grasped Sheryl's shoulder, giving her a hard shake. "Sheryl. Wake up." His nose wrinkled at the alcoholic fumes wafting from her. "Sheryl!"

She groaned. "Whatzup?"

Max shook her hard, alarm filling him. "Where's Noel?"

"Must've fallen asleep," Sheryl said, looking marginally more alert. Her eyes flickered, lifting fractionally, then slamming shut. "He's in his room."

"No, he's not," Max snapped. "How long have you been asleep? And why the hell are you drinking alcohol while you're minding Noel?"

"Not long." Sheryl glanced at her watch and turned pale. "Crap."

"When did you last see him?"

She'd conveniently avoided answering the drink question. Max itched to jolt answers from her, but he forced himself to take a step back to avoid throttling her. Hell, if his grandparents learned of this debacle, they'd make sure to inform the authorities.

"One o'clock. I made Noel a sandwich for lunch. After lunch, I put him down for a nap."

"You've been drinking since he went for his afternoon rest?" The words burst from Max before he could recall them.

"I found out my boyfriend was cheating on me. Not with a woman. He slept with a man. Says he's bisexual."

"I don't care," Max said. "Get up. Help me look for Noel."

Sheryl yanked a tissue from the box on her nightstand and blew her nose. "You're going to sack me."

Hell yeah. "You search the house. I'll check the barn. Noel loves visiting the kittens."

Sheryl moved with the speed of a geriatric snail. She clapped her hand to her head and moaned. "I have a splitting head."

Max snorted in disgust and strode from the room. He clattered down the stairs, grabbed a torch from the kitchen, and hurried outside. "Noel. Noel!" God, it was dark now. If something happened to his brother, he'd never forgive himself.

"Noel, where are you?" His younger brother adored playing hide and seek, and Max prayed he wasn't sitting in a favorite hidey-hole with a big grin on his face.

Along with checking the barn, Max walked the house perimeter and scanned every one of his brother's hiding spots. Where was he? If he didn't find Noel soon, he'd have to call the local cops along with search and rescue. His grandparents would learn of this and add this transgression to the long list they'd already gathered: drinking alcohol, womanizing, a single man with no experience of raising a special needs child.

"Noel! Where are you?" Max called as he jogged to the front of the house. He searched the garage, the interiors of his parents' Range Rover plus his Nissan, and the woodshed. Ah! The toolshed. He hadn't explored there yet.

"Hello," a feminine voice called from behind him.

Max backed from the toolshed and whirled to peer down his dark driveway. A woman walked toward him, her pace keeping time with his brother's awkward gait.

"Noel! Thank goodness. Where did you find him?"

"I found him on the beach. He was crying because he didn't know how to get home."

Max closed his eyes for a second, intense relief flooding him. "Thank you so much," he said with feeling. If this woman hadn't helped Noel, anything could've happened. "How did you learn where Noel lived?"

"I followed his footprints," she said, strolling closer.

"Max. Max. Max!" Noel said. "I went for a walk."

Max bit back his instinctive chiding words. He'd go over the rules about wandering off again tomorrow once Noel had rested. "You're lucky this nice lady found you." He held out his hand. "Maxwell Lombardy."

"My name is Sasha Mountholden," she said, accepting his handshake.

Now that his initial panic had subsided and Noel stood within sight, he noticed more about Sasha. She was tall, although he still had four inches on her. Her hair was brown with coppery highlights, and it was long and swept over her shoulders and halfway down her back in a tumble of curls. Gorgeous bright blue eyes returned his scrutiny with equal interest.

"Would you like to come inside for a hot drink? It's getting cold out here. Afterward, I can run you back to your car."

"We don't have a car. I mean, I," she said quickly. "I am visiting."

"Where are you staying tonight?"

Sasha frowned. "I am not certain. Once we found Noel, it was more important to help him get home."

"Thank you," Max said. "You could spend the night here. I have a spare room with an en suite."

A slight frown creased her brow before she nodded.

"I promise, I will not put a finger out of line or try to kiss you or molest you or do anything to alarm you."

She blinked before a slow smile made its way to her sexy, kissable lips.

Max cursed softly under his breath and kneeled in front of Noel for a distraction. He had no right to study her curvy shape, her long legs, or to pray for her to turn so he could view her rear. *Focus on Noel.* Much safer. "Are you hungry, buddy?"

Noel rubbed his tummy in answer. This close, Max spotted his brother's bloodshot eyes and the evidence of tears. "How about soup and toasted cheese sandwiches?"

"Yum," Noel said.

"I'm glad you're home."

"Can Shasha read me a bedtime story?" Noel asked.

"We'll see," Max said. Sasha hadn't agreed to stay the night yet. He understood a single woman might worry, but despite the temptation she presented, he intended to keep his hands off. A thought occurred as he stood and led Noel inside. "Did Sheryl have a long sleep?"

"She cried," Noel said. "Her cries hurt my ears." He slapped his hands over his ears in illustration.

Before they reached the front door, Sheryl flung it open and burst through. She carried several bags and juggled a flowerpot and her almost-empty vodka bottle. "I quit," she snapped, belligerence radiating from her. "You can send my final wages to my post office box."

Max considered several cutting remarks but bit his tongue. Sheryl beelined to her car, and Max couldn't hold back any longer. "You can't drive, Sheryl. You're still drunk. At least let me call you a cab." He enjoyed a beer or two himself but drinking and driving were a hot button for him, even more so after his parents' deaths.

"I don't need a taxi," Sheryl spat. "Your grandmother will learn you don't have an au pair for Noel." Nastiness and a hint of blackmail underscored her words.

Max admitted to a temper, and he hated people who embraced stupidity. Those like Sheryl, who blamed everyone else for their shortcomings. "Suit yourself."

"Bastard," Sheryl snarled. "I needed this job."

"You quit," Max countered. "I didn't fire you."

"I need a reference."

"Go to hell," Max said and placed his hand on Noel's shoulder to guide him past Sheryl.

"Is this one of your birds? Wait until your grandmother hears you're inviting them to the house now. This will thrill her."

"Sasha is my fiancée," Max said without a blink.

CHAPTER 2

An Awesome Adventure

"**N**o one told me you're engaged." Sheryl aimed for belligerent but wavered from side to side and was in imminent danger of toppling on her arse. The woman was in no condition to drive. He'd call the cops the instant she left. Luckily, he lived on a private road with only two residents—him and a businessman from London. His closest neighbor was away in France at present, so Sheryl was only a danger to herself.

"Because you're my employee, not my friend." Max shunted Noel inside and turned back to Sasha, silently imploring her to step across the threshold and not utter a contradictory word until Sheryl departed. Sasha glanced at him and raised an eyebrow.

The tiny tilt of her lips loosened his apprehension, and pleasure stomped out the rest when Sasha stepped boldly forward.

Sheryl cursed and stomped to her orange mini, although her swaying brought to mind a waddling penguin rather than a woman making a dramatic exit. She dropped her flowerpot while fumbling with the keys and swore again.

Max stepped farther inside, giving Sasha plenty of room should his proximity make her nervous. Her tilted lips grew to a sunshiny smile that lit her entire face and made her blue eyes glow. Then, she turned to shut the door, muting Sheryl's cursing at him, her car, and at life.

A red-blooded male, he scanned Sasha's form from the rear. He pursed his lips in a silent whistle of appreciation. She bore curves in all the right places. Well, hell. Why hadn't he met her six months ago?

"Are we staying?" her dragon asked. Her dragon's tattoo had moved around to Sasha's back and peeked above the collar of her shirt. *"Ooh! He likes us. He's staring at your butt. I bet he'd like my pretty bronze scales too. He told that lady we're betrothed to him. Why would he do that?"*

"I'm not certain. *The situation here is intriguing."*

"The Max man cares for Noel. You saw how worried he was when we arrived. The stomping lady failed to watch the child. She smelled of strong whisky. I think she drank instead of carrying out

24

her duties."

"We will stay," Sasha said, trusting her instincts. Pleasure rushed through her along with a raft of goosebumps and awareness. Why couldn't the dragon her parents picked for her look like Max instead of Bruceous? Granted, Bruceous wasn't ugly and took care of his presentation and fitness. It was his slimy manner and his adherence to the old ways that made her long to flee in the opposite direction.

"If Max man has a forked tongue and creeping hands, we will deal with him."

"We will," Sasha agreed. *"But it's best if we maintain our two-legged form right now. We must learn more. Where are we? How did we get here? How do we get home?"*

"I was wondering..." Her dragon paused and rearranged her form until she sprawled across Sasha's chest and belly. *"Even though we're lost, this adventure might be beneficial. It's perfect for an intrepid dragon like us. We can slowly investigate our plight while enjoying our freedom. The plants are different here, and we can learn more about what interests us. And, best of all, we will miss the meeting with Bruceous."*

"An attractive idea," Sasha said. *"The only part of this plan I don't like is that Mother and Father will worry. Our brothers too. Even though they boss us around and give us little independence, they do love us."*

"But not to take advantage of this opportunity," her dragon

wheedled.

"You're right."

"I'm going to heat soup for Noel. Would you like a bowl? I have tomato and lentil." He wrapped an apron around his waist.

"What's lentil?" her dragon asked. *"Never mind. I love to eat. Let's try it!"*

"Yes, please," Sasha said.

"Can you set the table, please?" Max asked. "The white bowls are in that cupboard." He pointed. "And the cutlery is in this drawer. Placemats in the drawer there."

"I love adventures," her dragon said with a happy sigh. *"Let's set this table thing."*

It surprised Sasha her dragon didn't mutter disdainfully about servant's work. It seemed she was ready to embrace this turn their life had taken. "Noel can help me if I get things wrong."

Max's smile when he turned to her was brilliant and full of approval. "Noel enjoys helping."

Sasha inclined her head and turned to Noel. "What should we do first, Noel?"

"Soup," he said helpfully. His nose had turned red, and his cheeks were pinker than when she'd first found him.

"How long did you walk?" she asked Noel while she opened the first of the drawers. "Did you get hot?"

Noel bobbed his head up and down, his round face solemn.

Sunburn. He required a tincture of aloe to calm his reddened skin. She'd search the garden later to check if Max had the plants necessary for her to make the sunburn cure. She set three placemats on the table and hesitated, unsure of what to do with them. In the end, Sasha shunted them toward Noel and turned away to gather the cutlery. She opened the drawer and slid it out to stare at the contents. The sheer number of implements had a slight sweat forming on her skin.

"Which ones do we require for soup?" she asked her dragon.

"Ask. We'll learn more about Max's character by his reaction. If he snaps or belittles us for our lack of knowledge, we'll know that underneath his smiles, there lurks a human who resembles Bruceous."

"You are wise."

"And beautiful. Don't forget stunningly beautiful."

Sasha tried not to laugh, but it burst from her in a wave of amusement and love of her dragon half.

"What's so funny?"

"Oops." Sasha thought fast. *"My brothers refuse to cook and would tease each other mercilessly if one of them wore an apron covered with rabbits."*

His eyes twinkled, but he put on an offended expression. "There is nothing wrong with my apron. It's Noel's favorite."

There was a considerable age gap between the brothers, and while they had the same blue eyes and black hair, their faces were different shapes. Aware she was drifting into rude with her staring, she focused on the contents of the drawer. "Which implements do we require?"

"The soup spoons and a knife each."

Sasha picked up three knives and dithered between two spoon shapes—one round and the other more elongated.

"*Pick the round one. There is more space in which to see our reflection,*" her dragon suggested.

Sasha bit back her hoot of laughter this time and picked up the rounder spoon. She took them over to the table.

"Placemats like this," Noel said and placed one in front of him and one opposite where he sat. He frowned at the third one.

"How 'bout we put that one here?" Sasha placed a knife and a spoon with each placemat. Noel immediately rearranged them, and she took notes for next time. "Great job," she said.

Max set a plate of soup down for Noel and another in the third space. He added a plate covered with singed pieces of bread and bubbling cheese. "The cheese is hot, Noel. Let it cool before you try to eat some."

"*Let's try the soup. Smells wonderful,*" her dragon said. "*I'm hungry.*"

"*Shush. I need to concentrate on correct behavior. We must appear as much like a human as we can manage.*"

"I can't place your accent," Max said. "Where do you live?"

"A small village on Perfume Isle," Sasha said.

Max frowned. "I've traveled a fair bit in Europe, but I've never heard of Perfume Isle."

"As I said, a small place. We couldn't wait to leave. I mean, *I* couldn't wait to leave. My brothers and I."

Max leaned forward, interest shining in his eyes. "How many brothers do you have?"

"Three, all older than me. They're bossy."

The corners of Max's eyes crinkled as he crunched on a piece of charred bread and cheese. "Older brothers do that."

"I like Shasha," Noel blurted.

"Thank you," Sasha said.

"I like Sasha, too," Max agreed with a wink at her. "Are you staying here tonight?"

"I think I will," she said, keeping her gaze meshed with his.

"Excellent. We'll talk later after Noel goes to bed."

"He likes us," her dragon crowed.

"Do you have the plant aloe in your garden?" Sasha asked with another glance at Noel. "Your brother's face is getting redder. I can make a balm to treat his sunburn."

"Thank you," Max said. "And thank you again for bringing Noel home. Sheryl shouldn't have gone to sleep and let him wander off."

"I don't like Sheryl," Noel said, splashing his spoon into his soup. The red liquid sloshed over the side.

"Ooh, that looks like fun. Let's try it," her dragon said.

"No. It's not polite. Mother would beat us if we didn't use our manners in company."

Her dragon sighed and rearranged her body so she could peer over Sasha's collar. *"You're right. The Max man has beautiful lips. I wonder if we could kiss them."*

"Shush," Sasha said to her dragon. *"Let's focus on Max and Noel."*

"Would you like to kiss Max?"

"Yes," Sasha said without hesitation. *"Now, please, let us concentrate."*

"Does...did Sheryl drink a lot?" Max asked.

Noel wrinkled his snub nose. "She smelled icky."

"How did I not notice?" Max muttered, and a frown creased his brow.

"He looks tired and worried," her dragon murmured.

"Yes."

"We will kiss him to cheer him up," her dragon said.

"He's worried about Noel. He doesn't need kisses," Sasha retorted.

"What man refuses kisses? And especially from us. We are gorgeous."

Sasha restrained her groan with difficulty. "Do you have someone to look after Noel?"

"No, that's my problem. We'll talk later."

"Of course," Sasha murmured.

"I like the soup," her dragon stated. *"Is it impolite to ask for more? I am starving."*

Sasha's stomach gurgled. Loudly. Max stared at her. Noel's almond eyes opened as wide as his rounded mouth. Then he giggled, an infectious laugh that had Sasha grinning ruefully.

"Pardon me," she said. "It's been a while since I ate."

Max rose. "I'll get you more soup."

He refilled their bowl and his too. Noel shook his head when Max offered him a second helping.

"I like the beach," Noel said. "Sometimes, I see dragons."

"Interesting," her dragon said. *"He saw us, but does he mean he saw others as well?"*

"What color are the dragons?" Sasha asked.

"Red," Noel said. "Bright red like Max's *broom-broom* car."

"We're not red," her dragon said.

"No, which means other dragons have found their way here."

"Noel likes to draw dragons," Max said.

"Wait until he has me as his model," her dragon said. *"He won't want plain old red dragons then."*

After the soup, they ate ice cream. It was cold on the tongue yet creamy to taste. Max covered the white ice cream with a hot brown liquid, and the entire dish had her dragon pleading for more.

"We will have more food later," Sasha promised. As a dragon, she used an enormous amount of energy, and earlier, she'd been too upset to eat. Ample food also made a curvy body, which had appealed to Bruceous. He'd told her so seconds before he'd groped her bottom. Bruceous was her best reason to lose weight.

"Have you finished eating, Noel?" Max asked.

The boy's head drooped, and his eyes kept sliding shut. He

didn't answer Max.

Max pushed away his plate and stood. "I'd better get Noel in bed. He gets grumpy when he's overtired."

"Do you have aloe? If we place the salve on Noel's face tonight, the sunburn will fade by morning."

"I don't know much about plants, but I have a torch in the kitchen drawer." Max turned to Noel. "Let's get you into bed."

"Will Shasha be here in the morning?"

Max glanced at Sasha. "I've asked her to stay with us, but it's up to Sasha."

"I can stay," Sasha said. "Noel, I'll be here, okay? Good night."

"Good night, Shasha."

Max sent her a grateful look and guided Noel from the room.

"We're lucky we have this offer of shelter," her dragon said.

"We are, although we could've slept outside if necessary."

"On the beach?" her dragon scoffed. *"That sand stuff might look pretty, but it gets everywhere. I am certain I have some in my scales because they're very itchy. We must wash my hide at the first opportunity."*

"We will," Sasha returned. *"Let's check the garden for aloe."*

"What about this torch thing? Who keeps a flaming torch in a drawer?"

"I don't know," Sasha replied. *"But it's not as if we require light to search the garden. Our night vision is excellent."*

A quick search of the backyard produced aloe plus several other useful herbs. The garden had once been well-tended but held a shaggy, unloved air now. Sasha's fingers itched to right the damage, but instead, she strode back indoors and set to work to make her salve. The familiar steps allowed her mind to calm and her thoughts to assemble themselves into a plan.

Not that she had any choice in the matter.

"You're right," her dragon said, having remained silent for a time. Unusual for her dragon, who had an opinion about everything.

"We must stay here and investigate," her dragon continued. *"It was luck to discover the boy. He's a strange wee fellow, but I took a liking to him. He's not a chatterer."*

"No, you prattle enough for all of us," Sasha said. *"Right, the salve is ready for application. Let's find Noel and sort out his face for him before he goes to sleep."*

She followed the faint sound of voices and stepped into a room with a narrow bed. Strange manmade things with wings obscured the walls, and several hung from the ceiling. A layer of dust covered them, a fact Sasha noticed because her mother would've sacked the servants for allowing laziness to defeat cleanliness. She made a mental note to clean the bedroom at the first opportunity because a young boy would not grow strong if he lived in a dirty room. Her mother's wisdom, yet again.

"And they lived happily ever after," Max said, closing the book he was reading to his brother.

"Hi, Noel. I've made something for your face. I bet your cheeks feel tight and sore."

He squirmed, his teeth biting into his bottom lip.

Sasha smiled and handed the cup of salve to Max. "Here, you go. Just rub it into the sunburned parts."

"I want Shasha to do it," Noel said, wriggling away from his brother.

Max sighed. "He's tired and grumpy. Would you mind?"

"Happy to do it for Noel."

She sat in the space that Max vacated and smiled at Noel. "It will feel cold at first, but it will take away the sting." With her fingertips, she gently rubbed in the lotion. A few minutes later, she sat back. "How does that feel? Better?"

"Yes."

"Tell Sasha thank you," Max said.

"Thank you, Shasha."

"Goodnight, Noel. Sweet dreams."

She stood and left the room. "We'll have a drink in the TV room," Max said. "I won't be long."

"What's a TV?" her dragon asked. *"Oh! Another adventure. Let's search for this TV thing."*

"We have no idea where to look."

"Ah, but now we have a chance to appease our curiosity," her dragon said, sounding a trifle smug.

Sasha pushed open several doors and peered inside. One appeared more formal, and once again, the furniture held a layer of dust. Not this room then. The next one seemed more promising. She took two steps into the room, and Max appeared behind her.

"Would you like a glass of wine?"

"No, I'd prefer a hot drink if possible."

"Tea?"

Since the beverage was familiar, she inclined her head. "That sounds perfect."

"The light switch is to your right."

Sasha had already worked out the light and pushed the button while Max padded to the kitchen.

Light filled the room, and her dragon clapped her hands together. *"I like it here. So many wonderful things."*

"It is fun having an adventure without our brothers breathing down our back," Sasha said with a smile.

"Yes! Quick, look at everything before Max returns. Everything," her dragon said, sounding wildly excited.

Curious herself, Sasha ambled around the room. Here, too, were signs of neglect. The area didn't require a spring-clean like the more formal ones, but her mother would've still tsked and chastised the servants. Books sat on a pile on the floor beside a faded chair.

"It looks comfortable," her dragon said.

"True." Sasha wandered on to study pictures on the wall. She recognized a younger Max and a very young Noel with a smiling couple. In another image, an older couple stood with them.

They weren't smiling as much as Max, Noel, and the couple she suspected were his parents. She drifted on to scan the tiny knickknacks and the bookshelf. The colorful books differed from those in her world.

"Pick up one. Let's read it," her dragon prompted.

Sasha picked two and sat on a chair. The first detailed the adventures of four bears. They wore clothes and went on escapades with their family.

"I love the pictures," her dragon said. *"Quick, Max is coming. Show me the pictures in the other book."*

Obliging, Sasha opened the second book, which featured a dog who liked to dig holes.

"We don't want a creature like that near our herb garden," her dragon said with evident disapproval. *"If that dog came to our garden, I'd eat him."*

"Ah, you've found Noel's books. He loves it when someone reads to him." Max set a mug on the small table beside the chair where she was sitting. He added a plate with two small, flat rounds that smelled intriguing.

Max placed another mug and food beside the shabby chair. He flung himself down with a hearty sigh. "I expect you have questions," he said.

"A few," she admitted, although she'd bet her questions weren't quite what he imagined since everything was new to her, and she was as curious as her dragon.

Max sighed again, his gaze going to the pictures on the wall. "My parents died in a motor vehicle accident six months ago. I lived in London at the time. Now, I work for an Edinburgh newspaper as a feature writer. Politics and current affairs," he added.

Sasha nodded and added another question to her list.

"Their deaths left Noel alone." His mouth twisted, and he sent her a wry grin. "You've probably already noticed the vast age gap between us. After I was born, my parents wanted more children, but Mum had several miscarriages. Then Noel came along—a total surprise for everyone. You'll have noticed he has Down syndrome. He takes longer to learn things, but he's such a cool kid. It didn't take us long to fall in love with him.

"Everything was great until my parents died. That left Noel alone here. I couldn't have that, so I returned to the family home and work remotely as much as I can. My problems grew bigger when my grandparents decided I wasn't a suitable guardian for Noel. Grandmother petitioned the courts for custody of my younger brother, citing the fact I was a single man, and given my career, I didn't have time for my brother." Max snorted. "Noel might have Down syndrome, but he's not as incapacitated as she made out to the court officers. He's a good kid and loves life."

"Your grandparents want to steal your brother away?" Concern filled Sasha at the idea of separating the brothers. It was easy to see they loved each other.

"My grandmother is the driving force behind the legal

maneuvering." Max pulled a face. "She never approved of Noel. But now, she thinks she can do better, and the social workers agreed with her."

"What happens next?"

"I thought I'd given Noel a safe and stable home life by employing Sheryl and taking on assignments that meant I'm at home most nights. If my grandmother learns of Sheryl's drinking and how she let Noel wander off, it will be another lever to use against me."

Max's shoulders slumped, and the shadows beneath his eyes denoted his fatigue.

"How do you know you can trust me?" Sasha asked, stating the obvious.

Given the circumstances he'd outlined, he was taking a risk by confiding in her—a stranger.

"I guess I don't. Perhaps," he said, "I shouldn't have told Sheryl you're my fiancée. If my grandmother learns Sheryl has left, she'll be asking questions."

"We have to help him," her dragon said. *"We can't let the evil witch steal Noel from his brother."*

"What can we do?" she asked her dragon.

Max sucked in a huge breath, drawing Sasha's attention. "The reason I'm telling you is that Noel likes you, and you brought him home. Your first thought was to protect him." He paused, hesitating. "What the hell," he muttered. "I know I'm asking a lot, and you might have other plans, but I wondered if you'd agree to the pretense of being my fiancée. If you'd be willing to look after Noel while I'm at work and help me persuade the judge I'm a decent person who is capable of looking after Noel. I can pay you for your time."

Sasha stared at Max, attempting to read his true character. So far, she'd approved of his actions and had seen the genuine relationship between the brothers. The inebriated woman had allowed Noel to wander off. She'd placed him in danger. "What would you need me to do?"

"I'd need you to look after Noel when I'm not here. He attends kindergarten at the nearby school three mornings a week. It's within walking distance, and I walk there with Noel, but Sheryl used to drive. You'd have to make meals for him, wash and dress him, and keep him entertained and happy. He loves learning new things, but he takes longer to master them than most children his age. Apart from that, he's a normal kid. Down children have low muscle tone, so my parents used to encourage him to run and play outside and visit the beach. I've continued with that as much as possible. He likes to draw and loves bright colors.

"My grandmother has visitation rights, and she has Noel every second Saturday. When she comes, you'd have to act as my fiancée. I'd be affectionate with you and maybe kiss your cheek and call you sweetheart. In return, you'll have room and board, and I can pay you the same wage I was giving Sheryl.

"Would you...could you pose as my fiancée? I know it's a fake engagement, but I believe it might help with my petition to get full custody of Noel."

"We should do this," her dragon said immediately. *"I like the funny child, and his brother seems like a decent man."*

"It would solve our problem of not having anywhere to stay, but we should try to return home. Our parents will be anxious."

"We have no idea of how we got here," her dragon said. *"All we did was our normal flight. What if we can't return? Besides, it won't hurt Mother and Father to worry about us. Max does not make me cringe in the same way Bruceous does. If we can help them, we should. It costs us nothing. In fact, he's going to pay us. We get food, a roof over our head, money, and an adventure."*

"I understand why you're hesitating," Max said. "You're a single woman, and you're alone in an isolated place. You're right to think of your safety."

"Is he joking?" her dragon shouted. *"We could take a measly human with one talon."*

Sasha winced even as she made her decision. "It is my honor to aid you."

Max stared at her. "You'll help?"

"Yes."

Max stood and closed the distance between their seats. He drew Sasha to her feet and hugged her hard before spinning her around with an exuberant whoop. "Thank you. Thank you so much." He set her on her feet and grinned at her.

Sasha's breath caught in her chest, and she stared at him. Heat shimmered through her, and sudden tension grew between them. Max gave a soft groan and leaned closer.

"You should also know that I find you attractive, and I badly want to kiss you."

"Ooh," her dragon whispered. *"I want that."*

"Me too," Sasha whispered aloud.

Max's eyes darkened, and he brushed a kiss on her lips. Quick and delicate, Sasha barely had a chance to record the intimate moment.

"If you keep staring at me like that, I'll kiss you again."

"Yes, please," Sasha said, and her dragon's anticipation resounded through her mind, an echo of the same words.

Max groaned and looked torn, but his hands landed on her shoulders. Their lips met again, soft at first, then Max settled in to kiss her in the exact way she'd seen Blaze kiss one of the dragons he'd courted for a time. Except this was much better because she was the one involved in the kiss. Max's mouth was soft yet insistent as he traced the seam of her lips with his tongue. When she gasped, he explored inside her mouth. It felt...

"Incredible," her dragon whispered. *"Do it back to him."*

Pleasure sizzled through Sasha as their kiss continued. Her breasts grew heavy, and she loved it when Max tightened his grasp on her and pressed her against his body. He was hard where she was soft, and because of their heights, they fit together perfectly.

Max drew back with a crooked smile. "Sorry, I didn't mean to get so hot and heavy."

"I enjoyed it," Sasha said, having no reason to lie.

"Just so you know, sex isn't part of the deal. I don't expect you to share my bed even though we're pretending to be engaged."

"*Aww,*" her dragon whispered.

Max took her left hand and kissed her knuckles. "Ah, a ring. As it happens, I have one. Wait there while I get it for you because my grandmother will expect a ring."

Sasha watched him stride from the room, her appreciative gaze on his form.

"*We're getting a ring,*" her dragon cooed. "*I wonder if it's a Marquess. They're the prettiest, you know.*"

"*We're borrowing a ring while we help Max and Noel,*" Sasha corrected. "*We can't keep it.*"

"*Are you sure? All dragons have jewels.*"

"*While that's true, we need to earn them ourselves or marry a rich dragon.*" Her dragon made her laugh. "*I'm certain Bruceous will shower us with jewels.*"

"*Not enough to put up with his shenanigans,*" her dragon stated.

Max strode back into the room, picked up her left hand, and threaded the ring onto her finger. It was pretty with red and white stones.

"*Aw, it's not a Marquess,*" her dragon said.

"They might not have them here," Sasha said absently.

"If you're wondering why I have a ring, it belonged to my mother. Mum gave it to me to give to my fiancée." He inhaled and closed his eyes briefly as if the memory gave him pain. "I was engaged to a girl called Bronwen at the time of my parents' accident. I loved her and thought she loved me in return. At first, she was very supportive, then she discovered I intended to look after Noel. She told me Noel had problems and would never be normal. She hated appearing in public with him. Not that Noel helped her opinion. He disliked her too, and on the couple of times we went out together with my brother, he misbehaved. When I wouldn't change my mind about Noel, she broke off our engagement."

"She sounds horrid," Sasha's dragon said. *"We must help Max."*

"We will help him," Sasha said.

"I like Noel," Sasha said to Max. "Don't worry. We will get along fine. I'll look after your ring."

Max shrugged. "I'm not worried about the ring. Are you sure about this scheme? My grandmother can be a bitch. She's hell-bent on winning custody of Noel. At the moment, we're waiting for the judge's decision."

"Does Noel like her?"

"Sometimes," Max said. "He senses the tension between Grandmother and me, even though we try to be on our best behavior when we're together with him."

Sasha patted his hand. "Don't worry. I can keep a secret and will do my best to look after your brother."

"Unfortunately, I need to travel to Edinburgh tomorrow. I was planning to stay overnight there."

"The trust goes both ways," Sasha said. "You must wonder if you're right to place your trust in me. I promise, I will guard Noel with my life."

CHAPTER 3

Sasha Meets a Human Dragon

A s was her regular habit, Sasha woke early. Dressed and presentable, she left her bedroom.

"*Hurry,*" her dragon said. "*We have to explore.*"

"That is not our primary mission," Sasha said. "First, we check on Noel. If he's still sleeping, we get to reconnoiter before we make his breakfast. Max promised to leave us a list of Noel's activities and what he likes to eat for each meal. It should be downstairs in the kitchen. If Noel is awake, we'll get him ready to face the day."

"*Can we go swimming? Can we eat the new food? Can we fix Max's garden?*"

"Yes, to all of that." Sasha grinned because the same excitement bubbled through her. This unknown world was full of exhilarating things. Even having an actual job and looking after Noel was thrilling.

She'd have her wages to spend, money she'd earned instead of depending on her parents.

"*Can we kiss Max again?*" her dragon asked. "*Can we flush the water in the privy? That was fun.*"

"I believe we're allowed to kiss if we're helping the pretense of our fake betrothal," Sasha said. "Do you want Noel to be awake or asleep?"

"*Hmm,*" her dragon said. "*Either. I like his funny face. Do you think our salve will have fixed his sunburn?*"

"There is nothing wrong with his face," Sasha snapped. "Max explained how some humans have this Down syndrome thing. It makes them different, but they're also the same. They like to play and eat food and learn interesting things."

"*We do too.*"

"Yes, so we can do all those things with Noel." Sasha pushed open the door, her gaze going to the bed.

Two eyes stared back at her. Noel sat up to reveal a striped shirt. "Shasha. You're here."

Sasha grinned at his eagerness. "Are you ready to start your day, or do you want to sleep more?"

"Not tired," Noel said.

"*Pull back the curtains,*" her dragon said. "*We need to see the day, so we can decide what to do.*"

"Food first," Sasha said when her tummy rumbled.

Noel's mouth widened as he stared at her stomach.

"My tummy is hungry," Sasha said. "Let's get you dressed. What do you want to wear today?" She drew the curtains, smiling as she spotted the morning sunshine. "We can play outside today," she told Noel. "Ah, your face is much better. Do you have a hat?"

"Yes." Noel bounced out of his narrow bed and almost tumbled when his feet caught in the covers.

Sasha grabbed him before he hit his head, and he beamed at her. "I like to go outside. Sheryl made me play inside."

"I see," Sasha said. "Where do you keep your clothes?"

"In here." Noel was dancing on the spot and crossing his legs.

"*He needs the privy,*" her dragon said. "*We should take him there.*"

"*Ooh! Excellent thinking.*" Sasha moved closer to Noel. "Bathroom first," she said, repeating Max's words of the previous night.

Noel sped from his bedroom and ducked into another room.

"Shout out if you need help." Sasha waited outside the door and listened for the right noises, following by the flushing apparatus she'd discovered earlier. It made everything disappear. So hygienic and less smelly than the privy back home.

Noel emerged, and Sasha directed him to the second room

they'd discovered. Water poured from the taps, both hot and cold, and soap came in liquid form from a bottle. Sasha helped Noel to wash his hands and face.

"I want to pick my clothes." Noel pressed his lips together as if he expected an argument.

"You can do that."

Noel's little shoulders relaxed. He trotted back to his chamber and opened a wooden drawer. He pulled out a bright yellow shirt in soft fabric. On the front was a picture of a green frog. From a second drawer, he picked a pair of trews in tough blue fabric. "Socks. Underpants," Noel said as if going through a mental list.

"Lucky for us, he seems to know what he's doing," Sasha's dragon said.

"And lucky for us, we get to make any mistakes with just Noel present," Sasha replied. *"I hope Max writes detailed lists because otherwise, this will be a tremendous adventure."*

"We're smart," her dragon said with her standard confidence. *"We can do anything. That's why they call us Sasha, The Lionhearted."*

With the help of Max's list, Sasha bumbled her way through a breakfast of something called rice bubbles—her dragon and Noel adored the sounds they made when coming into contact with the milk—and toast. Noel proved helpful, and since Max's notes said it was essential to keep Noel active, she decided to do a little cleaning before they played outside in the garden.

"Max makes my bed," Noel stated once they'd cleared the kitchen.

"Do you make Max's bed?" Sasha asked. Although they had servants, her parents had taught Sasha and her brothers to care for themselves and to keep their chambers tidy. Woe betide if Mother's room inspection failed her high standards. She and her siblings had learned to do it right the first time.

"No," Noel said, frowning at her.

"Max is tired," Sasha said. "If we do a few chores for him, he'll have more time to rest and play with us when he gets home." She didn't think he understood. "I'll show you how to make your bed today, and tomorrow we can do it before we come down to breakfast."

Noel's frown deepened, and Sasha understood what Max meant when he'd written his brother could become very stubborn. Max had also mentioned Noel enjoyed singing and music, so she tried another tactic. "I was going to share my bed-making song. My mother taught it to me to help the work go faster."

"What bed-making song?" her dragon asked.

"The one we're going to make up," Sasha said. *"About a silly old dragon called Bruceous who hated to make beds. I'm certain something bad happened to him because he was a nasty dragon."*

Her dragon guffawed so loudly a puff of smoke escaped from Sasha's nose. Sasha slapped her hand over her lower face to hide the evidence.

"Better start making up your ditty because Noel is watching us closely."

"Right, the song," Sasha said aloud. "I'll sing some of it on the way to your bedroom. Are you coming?" She set off before Noel had made up his mind. "There was a silly old dragon called Bruceous," she croaked.

Sasha's singing voice was terrible, and she admitted it, but if Noel loved songs and rhymes, she'd do her best.

"Who flirted with the ladies too much," her dragon sang.

"We can't sing that to a child," Sasha protested. Aloud, she sang, "Who never made his bed because he was the laziest."

"What's next?" Noel asked, staring at her in expectation.

"Yeah, what's next?" her dragon asked.

Ugh! Not only was she out of tune, but her rhyming was off.

"His mother proposed a bet. Bruceous would get a..."

"Set of goats?" her dragon suggested. *"Set of cows? Set of pretty combs for our hair?"*

Sasha sucked in a deep breath. "A pound of apple pies each week if he could make his bed."

"This is a terrible song. Look! Noel has clapped his hands over his ears."

"I know," Sasha said. *"What can I say?"* She winked at Noel. "Let's make the bed instead of singing."

"Yes." Noel wrinkled his nose.

Sasha burst out laughing. "You work on that side, and I'll stand here. Are you ready?"

Noel gave her a doubtful nod, but Sasha had an idea. She sang the instructions about smoothing the sheets and tugging up the blankets. Fluffing the pillow and folding his pajamas.

"There," she said. "That wasn't too bad, was it? Now it's time to see what Max says is next for you."

"Drawing," Noel demanded when they reached the kitchen.

"We should follow Max's instructions." Sasha scanned Max's notes, and the answer was anything as long as Noel was happy and challenged. Most of all, he needed to exercise instead of sitting around all day. "*Ah-ha!*" Sasha said. "Do you want to know what Max says in his notes?"

"Yes," Noel said.

"You can draw, but I have a suggestion. I'd like to explore the garden. How about if you come with me, and we'll look for butterflies? You could draw them. Will you help me look?"

"I like butterflies," Noel said.

"Great, that's settled then. Are you ready to go? Do you have boots to keep your feet dry? There's a heavy dew outside."

"What's dew?"

"I'll show you. We might find spider webs or some insects. I enjoy drawing them too."

Noel wrinkled his nose.

"Let's go. Are you warm enough?"

"Yes." Noel gestured emphatically.

"Do you want to bring your drawing paper with you?"

"Yes, please," Noel said.

Sasha helped Noel to find his drawing materials and placed them in a bag. Then, she led the way outside and into the garden. "Can you smell the fresh air?"

Noel sniffed loudly, making her dragon chortle.

"The weeds have choked the flower garden," Sasha said. "I love to grow flowers and herbs. While you're searching for something to draw, I can fix the garden and give the plants room to grow. Oh, look at the orange butterfly. Do you want to start with that one?"

Noel unpacked his bag and sat on the footpath, which thankfully, was dry. "The butterfly flew away."

"I can describe a butterfly," Sasha said. "Draw two big wings and a long, narrow body in the middle of the wings. They have two feelers coming from their head."

"Does a butterfly have eyes and ears?" Noel asked.

"I'm not sure. It doesn't matter. You draw eyes if you want. We'll save your picture for Max when he comes home tomorrow."

"Yes," Noel said.

"A young man of few words," her dragon said. *"Let's fix this garden. It will look pretty without the weeds and give visitors a better impression of the property."*

"I agree," Sasha said aloud.

"Who are you talking to?" Noel asked.

"I talk to myself," Sasha said.

"I am a dragon," her dragon said.

"Yes, but we must stay hidden while we are here," Sasha replied. *"It's not safe for our dragon here. Foremost, we must keep you safe while we work out how to get home."*

"Grandmother says people who talk to themselves are crazy," Noel said.

"Quite possibly," Sasha chirped, settling down to pull the weeds from the garden on the right hand of the steps leading to the front door. "This garden is full of weeds."

Noel sidled closer. "How do you know the weeds?"

"I like plants. My mother taught me about herbs and flowers. I enjoy making order out of chaos," Sasha said. "Last night, I gathered plants to make the salve we put on your face to take away the sting. You can make ointments and medicines from plants since they have healing properties." She tapped her fingertip on Noel's nose. "Your nose isn't red any longer."

A rumble grabbed Sasha's attention.

"What is it?" her dragon asked and moved up Sasha's neck so she could investigate.

"I'm not sure," Sasha replied. *"It sounds like the box thing on wheels that Max used to get here from his job. His square box has vanished, so he must've taken it back to his work."*

The black box came to a halt, and a door opened on the side. Sasha rose to her feet and plastered a polite smile on her lips.

The woman who exited had an oval face with few

53

visible lines. Sasha's mother would've approved of the woman's grooming—her smooth silver hair and subtly painted cosmetics—while her immaculate purple skirt and cream blouse shouted capable and classy. It was a pity her pursed lips and narrowed blue eyes contradicted first impressions.

"She looks grumpy," her dragon murmured.

"She does," Sasha agreed.

"Do you know the lady?" she murmured to Noel.

"That's Grandma," Noel said.

"The evil woman who wants to steal Noel," her dragon said. *"We must take care we don't give her further ammunition to use against Max."*

"Don't worry. Max has our loyalty."

"Hello, Noel," the woman said.

A man climbed out of the square box too. Sasha needed to learn the correct name for the transportation so she didn't appear stupid. This human was equally well-groomed and wore black trousers and a pale blue shirt, but he possessed better manners since he nodded a polite greeting at Sasha.

The woman hugged Noel, but he didn't enjoy the physical contact. He wriggled from the woman's embrace and returned to Sasha.

"Who is this?" The woman's gaze flickered up and down, her expression showing open disapproval of Sasha's black trews and plain shirt.

"Shasha," Noel said, taking Sasha's hand in his.

Sasha smiled at him before stepping forward to greet the woman and man. "Hello, I'm Sasha Mountholden."

"I thought Sheryl looked after Noel. At least she did until Max fired her," the woman said in a snooty tone. "That is unacceptable, which is why I've come to take Noel with me."

Sasha maintained a pleasant, non-confrontational smile while she and her dragon came up with a plan.

"We can't allow the woman to remove Noel," her dragon said. *"The woman is rude. She didn't even introduce herself to us. Mother would not approve of this human."*

"Exactly," Sasha agreed.

"Go and pack a bag for Noel," the woman ordered Sasha.

"I don't think so," her dragon said. *"This woman requires a set-down. Let's do it."*

Sasha didn't reply but held out her hand to the man who was frowning at the garden she'd started to weed and at Noel's butterfly drawing.

"Hello, I'm Sasha. Your name is..."

"Frank Cranshaw," he said. "This is my wife, Julia. We're Max's and Noel's grandparents."

"Ah," Sasha said. "Max has mentioned you. Why don't you come inside? We can have refreshments."

"We'll make that tea stuff and serve cookies," her dragon suggested.

"Perfect idea. We'll channel Mother when she has unwelcome guests."

Sasha ushered them inside. "Let me wash my hands, and then we'll have a chat."

"I don't think so," Julia said. "It's unacceptable to leave Noel with a stranger. Max doesn't spend enough time with the child. It's the reason we're petitioning the court for custody. It's not right, leaving Noel with Max. My grandson is never here."

"That's not true," her dragon said. *"Max loves Noel. He was most upset with that Sheryl woman."*

Sasha growled under her breath. *"It's obvious the Sheryl person has contacted the grandmother and told tales."*

"We must stop them," her dragon said.

"Don't worry. We will," Sasha said, a plan taking form. *"Thank goodness I placed Max's notes in my pocket. It wouldn't do for the grandmother to get hold of them."*

Sasha washed her hands in the bathroom and turned to see Noel loitering in the doorway behind her.

"I want to stay with you," Noel said.

Sasha ruffled his hair. "Don't fear, Noel. We'll have tea and cookies with your grandparents." She held out her hand, and Noel took it, but his expression remained worried. "Let's wash your hands first, then we'll have tea. Would you like to help me?"

"Yes," Noel said, confirming this with an emphatic nod.

Sasha dried his hands before they returned to the kitchen. She found Frank sitting at the kitchen table, his shoulders slumped.

"Easy to tell who wears the trews in this relationship," her dragon commented. *"He looks as if he's lost a tournament match, and everyone has jeered because of his defeat."*

Sasha guided Noel forward. "Is something wrong, Frank?" she asked. "Where is Julia?"

He offered a weak smile. "She went to the restroom."

The polite word for the privy, Sasha had learned.

"She's probably reconnoitering and gathering evidence against our Max," Sasha's dragon declared.

"She won't find anything incriminating," Sasha said. *"But just in case, I'll boil the kettle thing and make tea. I'm glad Max showed us that search thing to learn things."*

"I love Justine, The Smart Computer. Mr. Google is okay, too," her dragon said. *"Will we meet him in person? He seems most intelligent."*

"We'll ask Max later. Meantime, we have more important things to do for Max."

Sasha made tea and pulled a packet of chocolate chip biscuits from the cupboard. These, she set on a plate. By the time the tea was steeping and she'd set out the cups, Julia still hadn't appeared.

"Is Julia lost?" Sasha asked. "Should I go to find her?"

"I'll go," Frank said, rising abruptly. He muttered under his breath and offered Sasha another halfhearted smile.

"Well," Sasha said. "That is strange." She smiled at Noel.

"Would you like tea or milk?"

"Milk," Noel said. "And a cookie."

Sasha gave him the milk and placed a cookie on a plate for him. "Are the brown bits delicious?" She couldn't wait to try one.

"Yes, but they're not as good as Mummy's cookies. Daddy, Max, and me all liked them."

It was the most Sasha had heard from Noel and the first time he'd mentioned his parents.

"Maybe Justine, The Smart Computer, can help us make some for Noel. It won't be the same," her dragon said. *"But it might offer him comfort."*

Sasha agreed. She hadn't taken to Julia at all, and the woman's cold manner toward her and Noel didn't reassure Sasha. This was a woman who was trying to wrest Noel from Max because it would impress her friends and society. If she'd shown an ounce of love or concern for Noel, Sasha might've warmed to her more.

"You're not sleeping with Max," Julia said, sailing into the room like a fishing boat under full sail.

Sasha's eyes narrowed. "You searched my room?"

The woman brushed off Sasha's indignation. "Answer me."

"It wouldn't set the right example for Noel," Sasha said.

Julia's eyes narrowed in on Sasha's hand, the one bearing Max's ring. "Max gave you Hazel's ring!"

"We're engaged," Sasha said without flinching. If this woman wanted to intimidate her, she could think again. Sasha had trained with the high-ranked dames on Perfume Isle. Each social occasion where she'd learned to hold her own had prepared her for this moment. "It is an honor to wear Max's and Noel's mother's ring."

"When Sheryl told me of the engagement, I thought she was joking," Julia said. "Where did you meet?"

She and Max had agreed on a story, and luckily, Max had prepared answers for her. He'd told her to keep her answers simple and not to offer too many details. "We met when Max went on holiday to France."

"I see. Where are your clothes?"

Once again, Sasha was pleased Max had been thorough in his preparation. Sasha wrinkled her nose. "The airline lost my bag. They think the man at check-in mislabeled it and sent it to Hong Kong. Although how he managed this feat, I have no clue. It's most inconvenient. Max is picking up a few things for me while he's in Edinburgh."

Julia pursed her lips and appeared ready to launch into more questions.

"Offer her tea. Be the hostess and make her toe the politeness line," her dragon ordered.

"Excellent plan." Sasha beamed at Noel's grandparents. "I'm so pleased to meet you both. Won't you sit? How do you take your tea?"

Julia's brows rose. "We're having our tea here? In the kitchen?"

"Works for me," Frank said. "I've always liked this room. It's functional yet cozy. Hazel and John did a superb job with the renovations."

"I enjoy this room," Sasha said. "The colors are striking—the turquoise, the jade green, and the cream. They're perfect to offset the slate gray. It reminds me of the sea on a sunny day. Now, how do you take your tea?"

"A touch of milk with mine," Frank said.

Julia sniffed. "We're drinking from mugs?"

"Stop acting a bitch, Julia," Frank said. "We're family, and we're having a cup of tea in the kitchen where we're all most comfortable."

Julia's glare at her husband promised retaliation.

Sasha spoke fast to cut the tension. "Milk, Julia?"

"Lemon. Please," the older woman's politeness came a beat later than it should have.

Sasha plucked a lemon from the fruit bowl and cut several thin slices. She set them in a small bowl and pushed them across the table to Julia.

"Have you set a date for the wedding?" Julia shifted back to the previous discussion.

Sasha picked up her tea and took a seat beside Noel. "We thought about six months from now, but we have no firm plans yet. Max is keen to get married sooner, and I have no objections."

Julia snorted. "How old are you?"

"I'm old enough to recognize poor manners," Sasha said in an even tone.

"Max is using you to make the judge presume he's in a stable relationship and capable of bringing up Noel."

Julia's glare met Sasha's own. How dare she? And in front of Noel.

"I'm sorry you've made a trip for nothing. Max mentioned you have Noel for two weekends a month and reasonable visitation rights. I understood you mutually arranged the visits beforehand, though."

"You have a cheek! I have every right to see what sort of woman Max is introducing into my grandson's life. I was right to worry. You're too young for the responsibility of a child with difficulties like Noel. Max is *too young*, and I can't understand why John and Hazel would think he should be responsible for the boy."

Noel might be a child, but he understood the tension in the room.

"You've acted with the height of rudeness by turning up without following the correct protocol, you've searched my room and belongings, you've maligned Max—who isn't here to defend himself—and now you're insensitive to Noel. I am responsible for Noel and have Max's permission—my fiancé—to care for his brother. Noel is happy and healthy, but he won't continue in that manner if you continue to speak as if he's deaf."

"Well, I never," Julia said and sucked in a huge breath as if she was about to start again.

"Sasha is right," Frank said. "We shouldn't have arrived here without arranging the visit with Max."

"We have every right to check on Noel. Sheryl said you turned up out of the blue, and Max had never mentioned you before," Julia said.

"Sheryl was an employee," Sasha said. "Do you share details of your personal lives with people you employ?"

"There is something untoward here. I would feel happier if Noel came home with us."

"Noel has kindergarten tomorrow," Sasha said. "You would deprive him of the chance to learn and play with his friends?"

"Ooh, good one," her dragon said. *"Max prepared us well."*

"I guess he understands his grandmother," Sasha said. To Noel, she said, "You enjoy playing with your friends at kindergarten."

"Shasha is a dragon."

"He saw us," her dragon said. *"What are we going to do?"*

"Yes, I am," Sasha declared. "I am a fire-breathing dragon who understands you have no right to remove Noel from Max's care. Noel is safe with me, and we enjoy each other's company. I suggest you finish your tea, have a brief visit with Noel. Read him a story before you continue with your day. Noel and I have a routine. Noel likes his schedule, and you're upsetting him."

Frank stood. "Sasha speaks sense. It is time for us to leave and let Noel and Sasha resume their activities."

"This isn't finished," Julia said, bounding to her feet with such violence her chair toppled backward and crashed to the floor. "She's filling his head with rubbish. Telling him she's a dragon."

"I'm sure he doesn't mean a literal dragon, Julia." Frank sighed and offered Sasha an apologetic smile before facing his wife again. "It was wrong for us to come here and create this scene. I knew it before we left home but let you browbeat me into driving here. Julia, it's time for us to go. You might disagree with John's and Hazel's wishes, but it's clear to me Noel is in expert hands with Max's fiancée. Further, he likes Sasha, and you can't tell me he liked Sheryl. I swear I smelled alcohol on her breath the last time we met her for lunch. Goodbye, Noel." He winked at his grandson. "You be good for Sasha."

"Yes, Grandpa," Noel said.

"Sheryl looked after Noel perfectly," Julia argued, but she let her husband usher her from the kitchen.

"She lacks manners," her dragon said with an audible sniff. It was loud enough to draw Noel's attention. He frowned.

"It's okay." Sasha sought to reassure him. "My dragon is grumpy."

"Max says I get grumpy when I'm tired," Noel offered.

"I'm not a child," her dragon snapped. *"I don't require a nap."*

Sasha giggled without volition and hurriedly backpedaled when her dragon huffed. A signal for Sasha to step warily. "Shall we go outside again? You can finish drawing your butterflies. If you draw big ones, we can cut them out and pin them on the wall in your room. How does that sound?"

"I need my crayons," Noel said, wrinkling his nose.

"A suggestion," Sasha said. "Draw the outlines and color them when we come inside again. That won't take you long, but I can show you how to draw flowers or something else in the garden."

"Yes," Noel said. "Dragons."

"I thought we were keeping dragons secret," her dragon said.

"We are, but these humans assume Noel was telling lies and making up storybook characters. Note I didn't lie to them. I told them I was a dragon," Sasha said.

Noel scrambled off his chair, sprinkling crumbs everywhere.

"Next time, we'll get you a napkin," Sasha said, staring at the mess. "Never mind. We'll do our housework when we come inside. You can help me sweep the floor, okay?"

"Boys don't do sweeping," Noel said.

"Who said?"

"Grandma."

"Your grandma is wrong. Everyone should have a turn at sweeping and doing other jobs. It's how we learn." Sasha led Noel to the nearest bathroom and washed his face. "I can tell you about my family when we go outside. Would you like to hear?" She plopped a yellow hat on his head.

"Yes," Noel said, and his eyes sparkled in a way she'd already learned denoted interest.

Outside, Sasha settled Noel with his drawing book and pencils.

To start him off, she drew a giant butterfly. "This is how I draw my butterflies," she said. "If you draw them that big, we can cut them out and make it look as if they're flying through your room."

"Yes." Noel poked his tongue between his lips, his concentration total as he worked on drawing his next butterfly.

While Noel drew, she continued to weed, finding satisfaction in the manual labor. "I have three older brothers," Sasha said. "Their names are Blaze, Rafael, and Griffith. I am the baby of the family."

Noel glanced up at that. "You're not a baby."

"Parents always think of their youngest child as a baby, or so I've discovered," Sasha said. "My older brothers always tell me what to do, but they are still the best big brothers. Max is an excellent big brother," she added.

"I love Max."

Sasha plucked the final weed from the garden on the right of the front door and resettled herself to start on the left. "Max does seem nice."

"Can we go to the beach again?" Noel's intent gaze told her this was important to him.

"Do you like the beach?"

"Yes, Mummy and Daddy like the beach. Maybe we'll find them there."

"Ooh," her dragon said. *"Poor little boy. He's missing his parents."*

"Max is trying his best to fill the gap for him."

"But he can't be here all the time," her dragon said. *"Lucky for*

Max and Noel, we came along when we did, that it was time for us to have an adventure."

Sasha grinned. *"Lucky for us, you mean."*

"We should go to the beach," her dragon continued. *"We might sense the barrier or at least discover what happened and how we ended up here."*

Sasha nodded her agreement to Noel's request. "We can walk there this afternoon. But you must rest first. Max told me you need sleep."

"Don't need nap," Noel said.

"You might not need one, but I will because it is a long walk there."

Noel's forehead scrunched as he stared at her. "You could fly."

"No," Sasha said. "We'll walk since it's good to exercise your legs."

"Okay," Noel said.

"Oh, dear," Sasha said to her dragon. *"I didn't think he saw us that clearly. He must've watched our shift."* She finished weeding this small garden too and sat back on her heels with satisfaction. The front entrance appeared more welcoming already. Now that the weeds no longer choked the plants, the flowers would flourish.

"I've finished," Noel declared.

"So have I," Sasha replied. "Let's go inside and do a few jobs before we make lunch." Sasha stretched out a hand to Noel and helped him stand. "Make sure you pick up all your pencils and put them in the case. You don't want Max to stand on them and break your favorite ones."

"Noel doesn't move fast," her dragon said.

"No," Sasha said with a frown. *"I need to ask Mr. Google about that thing Noel has. What...ah, Down syndrome?"*

"Do we have this on Perfume Isle?" her dragon asked. *"I have never heard a mention of the syndrome thingie."*

"Many dragon families would kill a child they considered deformed," Sasha said.

"Noel has no deformities. He's different," her dragon snapped.

"Different but also the same as other children. He likes to do things and have fun. Loves the beach and misses his parents. He loves Max and is cautious with his grandparents."

"Because he senses the tension between them and Max," her dragon said.

The rest of the day passed agreeably. Sasha, with Noel's help, cleaned the kitchen until it sparkled. While Noel colored butterflies, she asked Justine, The Smart Computer many questions. With some pieces of kitchen equipment, she and her dragon experimented. They made lunch according to Max's instructions, and after pinning up the butterflies in Noel's room and reading an entertaining book with beautiful color illustrations, Noel had his sleep.

While Noel napped, she cleaned and dusted the room where she and Max had sat the previous night.

"Max is a fantastic kisser," her dragon commented.

Sasha turned warm all over. *"Yes."*

"We should do it again." Her dragon fell silent until Sasha picked up a pile of books. Her dragon scooted up Sasha's neck. *"Kissing books! We need to read those books."*

Sasha, whose mind had strayed to Max and his manly muscles, jerked at the excitement radiating from her dragon. "What?"

"Kissing books. We might learn more about sex if we read a kissing book. Wait! Let's ask Justine, The Smart Computer, right now. I'm certain human sex is similar to dragon sex."

Sasha shrugged, admitting to curiosity. She picked up the thing—a tablet, Max had called it—and typed in the question. Her dragon tattoo moved into a position where she could see better. Sasha clicked the first link, and music blasted into the room.

"Whoa!" her dragon said. *"Is that possible? Do our parents make those sounds when they have sex? Oh. Oh! That looks painful. Can a body bend like that?"*

Sasha stared wide-eyed at the screen when a second man appeared and joined in with the action. *"I'm fairly sure our parents don't do that. The gossip would've flown the length of the Dragon Isles."*

"True," her dragon said. *"Holy Bridget. I'm glad we escaped Bruceous. I do not wish to do any of this with him. Let's take a kissing book and read that. It might give us fresh information. The lady on the cover looks happy to be with the man."*

"All right. We'll read this one. The Taming of The Bad Boy. We'll start reading tonight."

The phone thing Max had given them rang, and Sasha started, her heart beating at double-time before she realized what was happening. She pulled the instrument from her pocket and stared at the flashing screen. "It's Max."

"Talk," her dragon commanded.

"No, remember Max said we have to push the button first." The ringing stopped, and the light left the screen.

"He's gone," her dragon said. *"What does that mean?"*

"I don't know. Maybe it will sing again."

Sasha continued dusting and tidying. She'd sweep the floors later if she could find a broom. If not, she'd ask Justine, The Smart Computer, how humans cleaned their floors. The computer thingie truly did know everything.

CHAPTER 4

Work Woes and Fantastical Beasts

M ax frowned at his phone, worry stirring in his belly. Noel had liked Sasha, but she hadn't known about phones or the tablet. He'd had to show her what to do, although she'd caught on fast and asked intelligent questions. The world was a small place these days, and even children in third-world countries understood technology. They had the internet in remote African villages. The more he pondered the wisdom of leaving his brother with Sasha, the more he worried over his decision.

Yet wasn't Sasha better than a drunk Sheryl who'd allowed Noel to wander off alone and become lost?

Despite his self-reassurance, his gut wouldn't settle. Although his grandparents meant well, his grandmother would coddle Noel instead of inspiring him. Noel might have challenges, but he was still a kid who wanted to join in and do the same things as his friends.

Max checked his watch and picked up his phone. He hit the number for Sasha and waited. The phone rang and rang, and his worry solidified into concern. Before he could ring again, one of the junior reporters knocked on his office door.

The perky blonde beamed at him. "The boss is calling a meeting. In five minutes. He wants everyone there."

"Just a quick phone call, and I'll be there," Max said.

The blonde hesitated, offered a grimace that held sympathy. "He's on the warpath. Circulation is down, and we have to fix it *yesterday.*"

Which meant he was in the firing line. Max sighed and shoved his phone into his pocket.

"I'd put it on silent if I were you," the junior reporter warned.

"Excellent call," Max said, recalling the last meeting when someone's phone had gone off during his boss's tirade. He placed his phone on vibrate, grabbed a pen and notepad, and followed the junior to their meeting room.

Everyone else was there when he arrived. Their grizzled boss swept in seconds later, resembling a mad bull on the charge. Max bit back another sigh because he didn't need to mind read to understand where this was going. More stories of the smut kind instead of factual reporting on current local affairs and items of public interest.

In different times, Max would've stayed in London or traveled farther afield to chase the kind of job he craved. His parents' death had changed everything. Now, he had to consider Noel. Yes, he could've let his grandparents take over Noel's care, but it wasn't what his parents had wanted. Noel deserved the best, and once Max had decided to accede to his parents' wishes, it wasn't fair of him to chop and change his mind. No matter how difficult his life became.

Mike Roberts, their boss, planted his butt on the desk at the front of the room. He was a rotund man with a dapper style despite his forceful nature. His signature bow tie—yellow and blue today—sat off-center, a sign of his perturbed mood. "Circulation is down. Our readers are deserting us in droves, which means advertising is down too. This can't continue. Tell me what stories are underway, and we'll see if we can spice up the next edition. We'll go around the room."

Mike's steely gaze settled on Max.

Max straightened, tension sliding through him. "I'm investigating local council corruption relating to the new housing project proposal."

Mike tapped his right foot. "How far along are you? Is the story ready to run?"

"By next week," Max said, mentally crossing his fingers. "My contact wants to go public, but he received threats that have scared him to silence. I need to work with him."

"Right. That's next week's lead story. What about this week?" He scanned faces, and Max's heart sank when no one spoke up. "Nothing?" Mike said, irritation coating his words. "Continue. What are you working on?" He pointed at the various reporters.

Some stammered through their replies, while others spoke with more confidence. None of the ideas was attention-grabbing, apart from a story about the vandalized statues in the town square.

"The scandal involving the cake-baking competition at the local agricultural show is what we want," Mike said. "But it's not necessarily page one stuff."

"Someone spotted Allan Briggs, the football player, in town," Sally, another junior reporter, said. "Rumor is he wasn't with his new wife."

"Excellent. Follow that up," Mike said.

"There's also speculation going around regarding the swingers at the squash club. They don't go there to play squash but to swap partners," their one photographer added.

Lucy, the blonde reporter who'd called him to the meeting, cleared her throat. "My sister swears she saw a dragon last weekend. She'd been drinking, but she took a photo of sorts."

Mike's eyebrows shot upward. "A dragon? You are kidding me."

"Ah, no." Lucy produced her phone and thumbed through

several apps. "My sister sent me a photo." She extended the phone to Mike, who peered more closely.

"It's not a clear photo."

"No," Lucy agreed.

"Where did she see the dragon?"

"At the beach. She and a group of friends had a barbecue on the sand. My sister was the only one who snapped a photo." Lucy hesitated before speaking again. "As I said, they were drinking, and knowing my sister's friends, there were drugs involved."

"Make discreet inquiries," Mike said. "Learn if anyone else saw the dragon. It might spark local interest, and a story like this will offer the buzz I'm after. A monster to rival the one at Loch Ness."

"We could do a series on local dragon lore," someone suggested. "To supplement the sighting. Maybe use dragons as the theme for the kid's corner?"

"Now you're buzzing," Mike said with approval. "Which beach was it where your sister saw the dragon?"

Max barely refrained from rolling his eyes. Dragons? What next? Flying saucers and aliens?

"Near Bamburgh," Lucy said. "The beaches are quiet during this time of the year. Not too many holidaymakers wander the sands."

"Bamburgh?" Mike's gaze speared to Max. "That's near you, isn't it?"

"Yes," Max agreed. "Although I haven't spotted anything out of the ordinary."

Mike stood and paced to the door and back. "When you get home after you've turned in the story you're working on, go for a few evening walks."

"I'm heading home tomorrow," Max said.

"No," Mike said. "I want you to finish your current article first and start on your next. If we're not pumping out stories, this paper will die a quick death, and we'll all lose our jobs. Understood?" His gaze nailed Max in place.

"Yes, of course," Max murmured, not having an option but to agree. His mind slid to Noel and the gorgeous Sasha, and his stress levels ratcheted up another notch. Had he made a wise decision the previous evening? Or had he let his libido lead him around like a fool?

The meeting broke up, and Max returned to his small office. Finishing the story meant staying away from Noel for longer. Placing greater trust in Sasha. No matter how attractive she was or how amenable to minding Noel, essentially, she was still a stranger.

His phone vibrated in his pocket, and he pulled it out to check the screen. His grandmother. Oh, joy. The temptation to ignore the call almost got to him, but it would only put off the inevitable.

"Hello, Grandmother," Max said coolly.

"Max, you didn't tell me you were engaged," his grandmother said.

Max groaned silently and pulled a face at the phone. One guess who'd told his grandmother. "We're not exactly on good terms at present. I didn't think my private life was pertinent to our interactions."

"You should have told me you've left your fiancée in charge of Noel," his grandmother said in a crisp voice.

"How do you know that?" Max asked, his mind jumping to conclusions that alarmed him. "Where is Noel? Do you have him?" Surely, if that were the case, Sasha would've called him. He'd taken a chance telling her the truth, but she'd impressed him with her deft handling of his brother and her levelheaded manner.

"Your grandfather and I visited Noel this morning. I intended to take Noel home with me since Sheryl is no longer in residence. It'd be easier for you if you didn't have to worry about Noel's well-being while you're in Edinburgh. Your fiancée refused to let Noel come with us. She informed me it wasn't our turn, and we had to stick to the schedule the judge gave us."

Max gave a mental cheer, some of his apprehension fading. "My fiancée has a name," he said, his tone calm.

"Sasha." His grandmother snorted. "She's young."

"The age gap between us isn't a huge one, and Sasha is the kindest, most levelheaded person I know. She's mature for her age and responsible."

"Be that as it may, I still prefer to know the people in charge of Noel."

"Noel loves Sasha, and she handles him beautifully."

His grandmother sniffed. "They were outside when we arrived. Keeping Noel quiet indoors is best, otherwise he becomes over-stimulated. Naughty."

"What were they doing?"

"Noel was drawing. Your fiancée was digging in the dirt."

Max's brows rose. Color him intrigued. An explanation for why Sasha hadn't answered the phone. They were outside. "Noel loves playing outdoors, and the exercise helps to strengthen his muscles."

"Surely he gets enough exercise at the kindergarten of his," his grandmother said.

"I'm only continuing with the program Mum and Dad mapped out for Noel's benefit," Max said. "Noel's doctors agreed with the exercises and activities my parents planned for him."

His grandmother sniffed—her default action to display her disagreement. "Noel told us Sasha was a dragon."

"She what?" The mention of a dragon had Max sitting up straighter.

"She's exercising his imagination, too, since she agreed she was a fierce dragon. She implied she didn't put up with inappropriate behavior. Max, she is too young to look after Noel."

Ah. A smile curled across Max's face. Sasha had bested his grandmother, and that had upset Julia. "I told you Sasha is mature for her age. Do you see me settling down with a youngster with no conversation? A giggly debutante?"

Julia sniffed again, louder this time.

"Grandmother, Noel is safe with Sasha." He felt better now, knowing that Sasha had stood up to his grandmother. Max firmly believed his words since Sasha had helped a small, scared boy who'd become lost. Not that he could offer the truth and give his grandmother a smoking gun.

"Sasha is wearing your mother's ring." A third sniff.

Grief sliced Max, and he forced it down. "Mum would've loved Sasha as much as I do."

"That's another thing. Your parents never met Sasha and didn't mention her to me. I'm positive they would disapprove of this quick marriage."

"They wouldn't approve of your actions either," Max snapped.

A sniff. "We'll be there to pick up Noel the weekend after next. Please have him ready."

"Of course," Max said, but his grandmother had already hung up. He pulled a juvenile face at the phone before making another quick call to Sasha. This time, she answered.

"Hello."

"Sasha, it's Max. I hear you're a dragon."

There was a slight pause. "Yes," she said. "I am a fierce and loyal dragon to Noel."

Max smiled at the truth that rang in her voice. "Thank you for resisting Julia's bulldozer tactics. I'd never considered her stopping by to visit."

"I have met far more formidable ladies. My mother is one," she said, her cheer radiating to Max. "I learned to stand up for myself as a child. Three older brothers who enjoy bossing me around also helped me to build a tough shell."

"Should I expect your brothers or parents to turn up on my doorstep?"

There was another pause. "I don't think so."

Something in her tone sounded off, and he filed that away to think about later. "Do you have questions for me?"

"No, Noel and I are getting along well. He's having a nap now."

"That's impressive," Max said. "I always have trouble getting him to sleep after lunch."

"I bribed him," she said with a laugh.

The rich sound hit Max straight in the groin. God, his grandmother was right. Sasha was too young for what he was thinking. She was an innocent as her kiss had shown him last night. The memory brought another inappropriate wave of heat charging through him. While she was innocent, she intrigued him in a way no other woman had during the last months. Hell, he had to concentrate hard to recall the last time he'd had sex. His brow creased. Ah, yes. The week-long trip to London before Christmas when he'd still been engaged.

"Are you there?" Sasha asked.

"Sorry." Max jerked back to the present. "My boss needs me to stay in Edinburgh for two extra nights. I'm sorry to dump this on you, but I can't afford to lose this job."

"Noel and I will keep busy," Sasha said.

Max stilled, waiting for more. Complaints. Something.

Instead, she said, "Is Mr. Google always right?"

Max grinned, curiosity about her background coming to the fore. "Not all the time, but mostly. You told me you don't have phones and the internet where you come from. It must be a small place."

"Not really." Her response didn't offer the information he craved.

Someone knocked at his door, and frustration leaped to life in him. He dragged a hand through his hair and glared when the person knocked again, knowing he had to end their conversation. "I'll contact you and Noel later tonight so I can say good night. Do you remember what to do?"

"Yes," Sasha said.

Her confidence made him grin. The woman *was* a fearless dragon, and he desperately wanted to unravel her mysterious façade.

CHAPTER 5

Fish Have Fingers?

"**B**each," Noel said the instant he woke.

Sasha grinned at the determined child. "Would you like to swim?"

His brows drew together. "Can't swim."

"You haven't learned?"

"Too little. Not strong," Noel said, matter-of-fact.

Sasha could see his disappointment in the way his shoulders drooped.

"Fix it," her dragon demanded.

"Do you have swimming clothes?"

Noel brightened. "Yes."

"Right. We'll get you changed and put lotion on your skin so the sun won't burn you again. I made a batch while you were sleeping."

"Are we swimming?" her dragon asked.

"No, we'll get Noel paddling in the water and let his confidence grow. I asked Mr. Google, and he mentioned swimming is an excellent exercise. It should help Noel grow stronger, but we must monitor him constantly and watch for waves that might knock him over and frighten him."

"We should study the area for clues to getting home," her dragon said.

"Probably," Sasha said. *"But I'm not ready to return yet."*

"Our parents will worry."

Sasha bit her bottom lip. *"While that's true, we will never get another opportunity like this to experience freedom. I want to read more of the kissing book. So far, it's fascinating. And we must learn more about Max. We enjoyed his kisses, and he doesn't pinch bottoms like Bruceous."*

"I agree," her dragon said. *"But while we should take advantage of the freedom, we should also watch for a way to return home. Options are never bad."*

"We can't leave Noel alone," Sasha said.

"Never," her dragon agreed. *"We cannot let the arrogant woman snatch Noel. She is the overprotective sort, and Noel would suffer. We understand what that is like."*

"Shasha!" Noel flapped a pair of bright red shorts in front of her.

"Sorry." Sasha helped him to change into his shorts and a T-shirt. She rubbed lotion on his arms, legs, and face before plopping on his hat. "I've packed a bag with towels, snacks, and drinks in case we get hungry. Shoes?"

"They're in the tiny room by the kitchen door," her dragon said.

"Right," Sasha said. "Let's do this."

The walk to the beach was much quicker when they traveled in a direct line. On this sunny afternoon, a few people walked on the beach, and farther along the sand, a family of two adults and two children played in the shallow water with a bright yellow ball.

"Where should we sit?" Sasha asked Noel. "Would you like to choose?"

He started running toward the water in his limping gait.

"Remember, we need our towels and clothes to stay dry. Why don't I pick today, and you can choose a spot tomorrow?"

Noel lurched to a halt and turned to her, his blue eyes bright. "We come tomorrow?"

"If it's not raining," Sasha said and walked farther away from other people. "We'll sit here. Now, I need you to listen. We have to follow the rules. Stay near me, and all the time, we watch the waves to make sure an extra big one isn't coming. Can you do that?"

"Yes."

"He would say that," her dragon observed. *"We said that, and we still misbehaved."*

A chortle escaped Sasha. It was all true. *"We'll hold one of his hands the entire time,"* she said. *"One little human kid won't get the better of a fierce dragon. Besides, two of us are watching him."*

Noel pulled off his T-shirt, and Sasha rubbed lotion on his pale chest.

"Leave on your hat. If it gets wet, it will dry in this sun."

Sasha stripped to her black underwear and her breast support. Since both were black and constructed of sturdy fabric, they resembled the swimsuits Mr. Google had shown her earlier.

"We're ready," Sasha said and led Noel to the water. He shrieked as the foam from a wave ran over his toes. It was difficult not to smile at such innocent pleasure.

"I might like a child," her dragon said.

Sasha snorted. *"Not if they're as naughty as we were. Mother says we turned her hair gray."*

"Untrue," her dragon said. *"Our mother is still young."*

"But she didn't have more children after us."

"Now that's true. I can sense the barrier, but it's a long way from here."

"Yes." Sasha pushed away the unease that shot through her. *"I still don't understand how we arrived here. The air turned heavy and thick. Seconds later, it felt normal again."*

"Wave," Noel shouted.

Sasha had already noticed it and gripped Noel's hand tighter at the wave's approach. "Right. Just before it reaches you, I want you to jump. Are you ready?"

Noel jumped too soon, but Sasha helped him to stay above the wave, and he shrieked with joy. Such a simple pleasure.

"Do you know how to blow bubbles?" she asked.

"No."

"Let me show you. First, we watch to see if a wave is coming. Right. No waves." Sasha made sure her grip was firm on Noel's hand and stuck her head in the water. She blew enormous bubbles and lifted her head. "Would you like to try? You take a big breath." Sasha exaggerated her breath, checked for waves, and repeated the bubbles.

"We learned in the pond near our home," her dragon said. *"It's harder in the sea."*

"Let him try." Sasha smiled at Noel. "Big breath. Check for waves. Bubbles."

Sasha observed Noel and grinned when he managed several bubbles. "Great job, Noel. Wait until we tell Max. Do you want to try once more before we get out to warm in the sun?"

"Yes."

The second time he managed two bubbles before a wave came, and Sasha lifted him above the surface. He looked startled, and Sasha braced for tears, but he giggled.

"You're very good at that. We'll practice more tomorrow. Do you know how to build sandcastles?"

He frowned. "No bucket. Forgot."

Sasha led Noel from the water, and they headed toward their

possessions. Sasha's skin prickled, and it wasn't from the breeze blowing over the sand. *"It feels as if someone is watching us,"* she said to her dragon. *"Can you see anyone staring?"*

"No. Wait. Let me shift on your body and study our rearview." Sasha's dragon tattoo migrated to a better position. *"I can't see anyone staring. I'll stay alert. You and Noel carry on."*

Sasha dried off Noel and pulled on his T-shirt since he'd had enough sun on his pale skin. "Are you hungry? I brought cookies and a bottle of water for each of us."

"The sun is reflecting off something in the trees over there," her dragon said. *"As if someone is using an instrument to see."*

"It might be nothing," Sasha said.

"Perhaps," her dragon replied. *"My senses say someone is watching us. I wish we could investigate, but we can't leave Noel."*

"Noel, would you like to make a dragon on the sand?" Sasha asked.

Noel cocked his head. "Don't know how."

"Lucky for you, I'm good at making dragons." Sasha stood and dusted off her backside. She wandered a few steps and plucked a piece of driftwood from the sand. Using the stick, she drew the shape of a dragon. "Now, you can help me. We need to scoop up handfuls of sand and fill in the lines. It's like coloring a picture, but we're using sand instead of your crayons or pencils."

By the time they'd spent an hour playing in the sand, Noel was lagging, and Sasha decided it was time to leave.

"Wanna stay," Noel said.

"Not today," Sasha said firmly. "I'm turning pink from the sun. Tomorrow morning you have to go to kindergarten, but we can visit the beach in the afternoon."

"Promise?"

"Yes," Sasha said. "We will come tomorrow. What would you like for dinner?"

"Fish fingers," Noel said.

"What are fish fingers?" her dragon asked. *"Do fish have hands? Are they different here?"*

"No." But Sasha wasn't sure. *"We should ask Justine, The Smart Computer."*

"It sounds barbaric to cut fingers off a fish," her dragon said. *"Wouldn't they miss them?"*

"You'd think," Sasha replied. *"Can you spot anyone watching us?"*

"No, but I see the flash from the watching glasses again."

Once they arrived home, Sasha showered Noel and investigated Max's list. She pulled a face. "Justine, how do I make an online call?" She and her dragon listened intently to the reply. "That doesn't sound too difficult."

"I'm hungry," her dragon said. *"What are we having for dinner?"*

Sasha consulted the list. "Justine, what are fish fingers?"

"Pieces of fish pressed into strips and coated with breadcrumbs," a feminine voice said from the computer.

Sasha had always loved cooking and found she enjoyed it even more when she didn't have her mother—or the servants who'd been with the family since she was a baby—peering over her shoulder. Usually, with many comments about her methods and that she was doing everything the wrong way. Here, she could make mistakes, and no one learned of them apart from her and her dragon. Noel, too, since the three of them had to deal with her blunders.

Even the video call went okay, although she cut Max off the first time.

"Sorry," she said, wrinkling her nose. "I hit the wrong button."

Max laughed, his arresting face clear on the screen. "Now, where is Noel?"

"Here!" Noel said from his bed. He wore his pajamas and sat tucked up in bed. "Shasha is teaching me to swim."

"Really?" Max sounded surprised, but she thought in an appreciative way. "How did you get on?"

"I blew bubbles. Three times. But we have to watch for waves."

"I see," Max said. "What else did you do?"

"Butterflies. Drew them. Look!"

"I can't see, buddy. Ask Sasha to shift the screen to show me."

"Oh!" Sasha said. "I can do that. No, you stay there. I'll bring Max back to you once I show him your butterflies, which are brilliant, by the way. I bet Max thinks so too." She carefully lifted the screen and directed it toward the sweep of bright orange, yellow, and red butterflies that decorated Noel's room.

"Did you draw those?" Max asked when Sasha returned the tablet to Noel.

"Yes," Noel said, excitement sparkling in his eyes. He'd caught the kiss of the sun today and wasn't as pale or blotchy.

"What else did you do?"

"Dragon sandcastle," Noel said, beaming. "It was big."

"Do you like dragons?" Max asked, and Sasha picked up the strange note in his voice.

"I like Shasha."

"Oops," her dragon said. *"He definitely saw us before we shifted."*

"Too bad," Sasha said. *"We'll deny everything. That is the wisest course to follow since there don't appear to be other dragons here. Everyone we've sighted is human."*

"I like Sasha, too," Max said. "You be a good boy for Sasha, and I'll be home in a few days. Has Sasha read you a story?"

"She told me a dragon story from her head."

Max grinned. "All right. You go to sleep while I talk to Sasha. She'll come and check on you once we're finished. Okay?"

"Night, Max," Noel said, settling in his bed.

"Good night. Sweet dreams, Noel."

Sasha lifted the tablet and stared at Max. He smiled at her, a genuine smile with wide lips and sparkling eyes. Approval was the dominant trait in his expression, yet the feminine part of her identified the masculine interest.

"Why don't you take the tablet to the kitchen and make a cup of tea? I'll do the same, and we can chat while we drink." Once she'd followed his instructions regarding the tea, he directed her to what he called the family room. It was the one in which they'd sat the previous evening.

"If I was there in person," Max said, "I'd kiss you. You've worked wonders with Noel in one day. He's excited about everything he did today. You've taught him new things and engaged him. On top of that, you faced down our grandmother and won since she didn't remove Noel. Thank you so much. The first thing I'm going to do when I see you in person is kiss you and give you a big hug."

"Yes, please," Sasha said.

Max stared at her, his eyes turning a deeper blue. The look on his face had her pulse racing faster while her dragon released a faint moan.

"Damn," he whispered. He shook his head, took a deep breath, and changed the subject. "There is a swimming pool near the kindergarten. You can take Noel there so you won't have to watch for waves. He's never mentioned swimming before. It never occurred to me, and it should've considering we live so near to the beach."

"It's no problem."

"Do you have a swimsuit?"

"No," Sasha said. "I swam in my underwear. No one stared at me."

"I would've noticed," Max cleared his throat. "My mother was of a similar height and size to you. I haven't managed to enter my parents' room to clear out their clothes. Why don't you take what you can use?"

Sympathy washed through Sasha. "I have time to deal with the room if you want. I can keep aside the personal trinkets you might wish to keep." She hesitated. "I understand if you don't want a stranger to do this for you. There is no rule to say you must do this immediately."

"How did you get so wise at your age?" Max asked, his voice thick and his eyes now glassy with emotion.

"We have always been wise."

His brows rose. "We?"

"I mean I," Sasha said without an explanation. "Also, you haven't known me for long. It's understandable if you don't trust me yet. Think about it. As I said, there is no hurry."

"I trusted Sheryl since she looked after Noel when my parents were alive. Yet it turns out she's a drunk and a spy for my grandmother. I had my suspicions, but I wasn't positive. In the short time you've been with Noel, his mood has improved. He's excited about new things. You're patient with him, and you don't treat him like a moron because he's different. And, you helped a lost child when I'm certain you had other plans."

Sasha shrugged, discomfort rippling through her. "Anyone would've done the same thing."

"No, they wouldn't," her dragon said.

"Not everyone," Max said. "As a reporter, I see the worst of people. The best too, but it's the horrid things that stick with me. As my other grandmother used to say, *you're a treasure.* Go ahead and clear my parents' room. I'll pay you a little extra for the help."

"That's unnecessary," Sasha said. "You're already paying me to look after Noel. I'll take a few clothes in exchange. That is fair."

"He doesn't realize the freedom and safety he has offered us is beyond any money he could pay," her dragon said.

"Exactly," Sasha replied.

Max sighed. "I guess I'd better go since I still have work to do before I can sleep."

"I might bake some cookies."

"You'll find the ingredients in the pantry. If there is anything you need, write a list, and I'll pick the stuff up on the way home. Talk to you again tomorrow?"

"Definitely," Sasha said. "Both Noel and I will look forward to it."

"Goodnight, Sasha."

The screen flickered, and Max had gone before she could reply.

"He likes us," Sasha said.

"As he should," her dragon declared. *"We are gorgeous, and we're smart. We're also trustworthy. He'd be an idiot not to want us as a friend. We are Sasha, The Lionhearted!"*

Sasha grinned and rose, ready to work in the kitchen.

"There's no reason not to accept the truth because we are beautiful and a catch. Why do you think Bruceous is chasing us so hard?"

As always, her conceited dragon had the last word. Sasha wasn't about to argue over Bruceous's intentions and spoil her buoyant mood.

CHAPTER 6

A Family Date

S asha's first day with Noel set the pattern for the rest of the week. When Noel wasn't at kindergarten, she completed tasks around the house and got Noel to help with minor jobs. She took him to the pool for more swimming lessons and ended up teaching three children of the same age as Noel how to swim while their parents watched. One child invited Noel to a birthday party, and Max was as excited as Noel when he learned of the coming event. Sasha was also slowly making friends with mothers she met during kindergarten drop-off and at her impromptu swimming lessons.

"Max must be older than you," Rachel, one of her new friends, said at the outdoor cafe overlooking the pool. "Several of the single women have had their eye on Max."

"A few years older," Sasha said with a shrug while her dragon grumbled about the other women. Sasha ignored her dragon.

"That's such a gorgeous ring. I adore colored stones," Rachel continued. "Coffee?"

"Yes, please," Sasha said. "This ring used to belong to Max's mother."

Rachel shuddered. "I'm not sure I would want his mother's ring."

"Why not?" Sasha attempted to keep the sharp note from her voice and failed. "Max and Noel loved their mother, so the ring has sentimental value for them and, therefore, for me too. Besides, you're right. The ring is pretty. I like it very much." Now that was the truth. She and her dragon enjoyed seeing the envy on the faces of those single women.

"Coffee," Rachel said. "Let's grab a seat near the kids so we can monitor them."

Ten minutes later, Sasha picked up their coffee while Rachel grabbed the plate bearing the slice of chocolate cake they'd decided to split.

"Did you meet Max's parents?" Rachel asked.

"She's a nosy one," her dragon complained.

"It's best if we answer her questions. She seems like the chatty type who might gossip."

"Ah, you mean she'll pass on the information so we don't have to

repeat ourselves."

"Exactly," Sasha said and sipped her coffee before she answered Rachel. "No, I never met Max's parents. They sound like amazing people. I know Max and Noel miss them dreadfully."

"I understand Max's grandmother is suing for custody of Noel," Rachel said.

"Enough," her dragon said.

Sasha's mouth firmed. "I don't know anything about that."

Rachel looked as if she didn't believe Sasha, but she ceased her probing questions. "What are you buying Tiffany for a birthday present?" she asked instead.

"For the party?"

"Yes. That child has everything. It's difficult to know what to get her."

"Max said he'd pick up something in Edinburgh," Sasha said.

"Lucky you." Rachel pulled a face. "My husband would never offer to help in that way. You'd better enjoy it while you can. Men change after marriage."

Sasha knew nothing about that, so she merely smiled and sipped her coffee again.

"I like this coffee stuff," her dragon said. *"It's much tastier than those fishes' fingers."*

"I have to agree," Sasha said absently.

Their chat turned more general, and Sasha listened carefully as Rachel mentioned the various things that were happening in the area. Apart from birthday parties and school events, there was an upcoming agricultural day and a concert, plus a garden party. Sasha stored the information and ignored her dragon, who was asking enthusiastic questions. They needed to save their curiosity for Justine since the lady in the computer seemed knowledgeable regarding everything.

With the coffee and cake finished Rachel stood. "I guess it's time to get back home. I have laundry and a million other jobs I've been putting off. What about you?"

"I'm cleaning a room each day. I expect Noel will want to go to the beach. We end up going most days. We both enjoy the walk there and the sea air."

"Have you seen the dragons everyone is talking about?"

"What dragons?" Sasha asked.

"Dragons?" her dragon asked. *"We have seen none."*

"A group of teenagers saw one the other night. Secretly, I suspect they were doing drugs, but who knows? It's all over the district, and each night people are hanging out in the beach car park to look for dragons."

"I see," Sasha said. "Is it safe to go to the beach?"

Rachel snorted. "The day I see a dragon flying through the sky is the day I cut back on drinking."

"I'm tempted to help Rachel to reduce her drinking," her dragon said immediately. *"Where does she live?"*

Sasha barely contained her hilarity because she'd experienced the same yearning to scare this opinionated woman. She pushed her coffee cup away and rose. "It's time for Noel and me to move. I need to put on the chicken for dinner."

Five minutes later, they were on their way home.

"Why do we walk?" Noel asked.

"Two reasons," Sasha said. "I can't operate a metal box, and exercise is necessary to build our muscles."

"Car or vehicle," her dragon corrected.

"Car, right," Sasha said aloud. "I can't drive a car."

"Me neither," Noel said.

They turned into the driveway to find a car parked in front of the house. Sasha inhaled, and her pulse raced faster at the familiar scent.

"Max is home," she said.

Sasha opened the front door for Noel.

"Max. Max!" Noel shouted.

"In here, champ," Max called.

Sasha sucked in a quick breath as eager to see Max as Noel. They'd spoken each night after Noel had gone to sleep, and she liked him a lot.

"Enough to practice more kissing?" her dragon asked.

Heat surged to Sasha's cheeks, but she didn't hesitate in her answer. *"Yes."*

When she entered the kitchen, Noel was talking so fast Sasha had problems keeping up. Max grinned and winked at her.

"Wow, you've been having lots of fun. How would you and Sasha like to go out for dinner tonight?" Max glanced at her as he asked.

"I've taken out a chicken to roast, but I can cook that tomorrow night." Sasha bounced on her toes, keen anticipation at the treat filling her chest with lightness.

"From what Noel tells me, you've been cooking a lot. He says your chocolate chip cookies are delicious. He'll be getting a fat tummy."

"I don't have a fat tummy." Noel lifted his T-shirt to peer at his stomach, his tongue sticking out as he stared at his belly.

No longer a pasty white, his skin was pale gold, and the child had lost a little weight. Sasha thought Noel looked happy and healthy.

"No, you don't," Max confirmed, the corners of his eyes creasing with silent laughter. "I thought we'd have fish and chips and mushy peas. Have you had that before?"

Sasha shook her head. "Is it tasty?"

"Yes. And afterward, we could walk on the beach or maybe around the castle grounds."

"Yay!" Noel shouted. "I like the castle and the beach."

"Why don't I get you showered and changed?" Max asked. "Sasha can have some time to herself and a leisurely shower. We'll leave in about an hour. Is that all right with you?"

"Perfect. What should I wear? Oh, and while I remember, did you get Noel a present to take for Tiffany for her birthday party?"

"Jeans or something casual is fine," Max replied before pulling a face. "I forgot the present. The shops will be open when we go into Bamburgh. The bookshop might have something suitable. What do little girls like?"

Sasha shrugged. "I enjoyed playing with my brothers' toys. Maybe a book."

"A kite," her dragon said. *"I bet she doesn't have one of those."*

"Noel and I have been reading a book about a boy who made a kite. Could we buy a kite somewhere, plus a copy of the book we're reading? The book has girls and boys in it."

"That might work," Max said. "It sounds as if Noel would like a kite."

"A dragon kite," Noel said.

"Perhaps a book about dragons," Max said. "Funny, I've been hearing a lot about dragons lately."

"Sasha is a dragon," Noel said.

"She is fierce," Max said, sending her a wink. "Let's get you in the shower."

Max ushered Noel away, leaving Sasha in the kitchen.

Her dragon climbed her neck to peer after them. *"I wonder why we didn't scare Noel. Most humans fear dragons, even the humans in the village on Perfume Isle. Remember that girl we met at the stream? Her mother wouldn't let her play with us."*

"Noel differs from other kids," Sasha said. *"Maybe his differences allow him to accept our variations. Max doesn't believe Noel saw a*

dragon, which is for the best. For our safety, we need to blend. I wish we could investigate the barrier more closely, though."

"Now that Max is home for a while, we might have an opportunity to sneak outside and fly out to sea," her dragon said.

Sasha hesitated before replying, *"Part of me wants to do that, while the other part of me prefers to stay right here. What if the air is thick again, and we can get through? We wouldn't have any way of returning to Max and Noel."*

"I understand your fears because mine are similar. Besides, I want us to kiss Max again and maybe do some of those other things we've read of in the kissing books."

With her thoughts a thousand miles away from choosing something to wear, she picked up the chicken, placed it on a platter, and set it in the refrigerator.

"Such a handy gadget," her dragon said, pulling Sasha's mind away from Max and kissing. *"I'd miss the useful, timesaving things they have here on the mainland. Their lives are so different."*

"Do you not want to return to Perfume Island?"

"Yes and no," her dragon said. *"That's not a straightforward question. I miss our family, but the endless social occasions and stupid dragons like Bruceous I can do without. The world here seems richer, and women of our age have more freedom. I could live here, but I'd have to fly. We haven't done that since we arrived."*

"I miss flying too."

"Sasha, you're still here," Max said.

"Problem?" she asked.

"Yes," Max said, walking straight to her. He drew her into his arms and grinned, his blue eyes twinkling. "I haven't kissed you yet." With that said, he settled his lips on hers.

Sasha curled her hands around his biceps and parted her lips, having more of an idea of what to do and what she wished to try this time. He groaned and pulled her closer until her breasts brushed the muscles of his chest. While dragons were casual with their nudity, manners still applied, and they never stared at sexual parts. Max's man-part—his cock— pushed against her lower body, and Sasha enjoyed the pressure. The kissing books had been enlightening and bolstered the scant information she'd received from her mother and overheard from her brothers. At this moment, everything made sense.

Max slid his tongue against hers, and her stomach flip-flopped at the intimacy of the action. She enjoyed his touch very much and was eager to try more. Unfortunately, Max pulled away, and Sasha groaned in a muffled protest.

Max laughed and kissed the tip of her nose. "If I keep kissing you, we'll never get to dinner, and Noel will be most upset. Noel wants to explore the castle grounds since he informs me he goes to the beach most days." Max sobered. "Sasha, I don't deserve you. Noel and I appreciate everything you've done. The house looks fantastic, both inside and out. I noticed the work you've done in the garden and how clean the interior of the house is now. Noel tells me he helps with chores."

Pleasure shimmered through Sasha because Max had noticed and genuinely valued her efforts. "I try to teach Noel something new every day. He enjoys doing minor tasks."

"You've made work into a game for him. He looks so well and is happy. He's made more friends, and he has a social life. I could tell he was doing well when I spoke to him each night, but seeing him in person—the difference in him is amazing. His room too. Thank you for thinking of giving him a picture of Mum and Dad."

"He misses them. I know what it's like to miss family."

Max smiled. "Your family is welcome to visit you here. We have spare rooms if they'd like to stay for a few days."

"Thanks for the thought," Sasha said without further comment.

"Are you changing? Not that you don't look incredible in what you're wearing," Max said easily. "I'm discarding this suit and putting on a pair of jeans and a casual shirt."

Sasha nodded. "I'll meet you down here in ten minutes." True to her word, she had a quick shower before changing into a denim skirt, a red T-shirt, and the leather jacket she'd discovered in Max's mother's wardrobe. His mother seemed to have kept clothes for years. Sasha didn't know much of the fashions here, but after asking Justine, The Smart Computer, and checking on what the other mothers were wearing, she'd learned the clothes were perfect. She wore her own sandals, the pair she'd carried from Perfume Island.

"That was quick," Max said.

"I told you ten minutes."

"Most women of my acquaintance take much longer to get ready," Max said. "Mum was always late, and the two women I've dated recently were just as bad."

"Are you dating anyone now?" Sasha asked. Once the words emerged, she cursed under her breath.

"No," Max said, taking her hand in his. "We're engaged, even if it is a pretense for everyone else. That means there is just you in my life."

"Is that why you kissed me?" Sasha loathed being an obligation.

"Hell no," Max said without hesitation. "I kissed you because I wanted to. First, I promised you a huge kiss, and believe me, you deserve a lot more than a kiss by way of thanks for everything you've done for Noel and for me. Second, I'm attracted to you." His gaze held hers as he said the words. "Very attracted."

Sasha swallowed, feeling uncharacteristically shy. "Thank you."

"You're welcome. Are you ready, Noel?"

"Yes!"

Max shepherded them out to his vehicle. He opened the rear door, and Sasha watched as he settled Noel in something he called a kiddy seat. Max explained it was a law for children to have this special seat. With Noel seated, he escorted her around to the other side and opened the door for her. She slid inside, uncertain of what to do next.

Max jumped into the car and pulled a silver handle, which revealed a black strap, and he clicked it into another object.

"We have one," her dragon said, her tattoo peeking above the collar of Sasha's shirt. *"We should do the same."*

Sasha copied Max's actions and succeeded in not making a fool of herself. Sasha and her dragon had quizzed Justine, The Smart Computer, about these cars, so they knew what would happen next. A throaty roar signaled the machine waking, and in the next minute, they were off.

"Whee! It's almost as much fun as flying," her dragon said.

"How come you don't drive?" Max asked.

"I've never learned." Nor had the need, considering she could fly anywhere she wished to travel.

"I didn't think to tell you. There is a bus stop not far from the end of our road. If you and Noel want to travel farther afield and perhaps visit the castle or the shops, you can catch the bus. I'll leave you some change for the bus fare."

"Thank you," Sasha said, taking a mental note to ask Justine, The Smart Computer, about catching the bus. It sounded like an adventure she'd enjoy.

"That's the bus stop there." Max pointed to a seat with a tiny roof over the top—a shelter of sorts from the elements, Sasha guessed.

Sasha found lots to study on the drive to the restaurant. Another novelty since food sellers on Perfume Isle rarely had tables and seats for their customers.

Max parked his car and climbed out. Sasha observed him, so she understood what to do and how to exit. She managed it perfectly while Max helped Noel. Once they were ready, Max took Noel's hand and held out his other for her.

She hesitated.

"I don't bite," Max said.

"The kissing books have a little biting," Sasha said without thinking. "Some ladies seem to enjoy it."

"Kissing books?"

"The ones with the ladies and men on the front. I've been reading them."

Max's brows rose. "I see."

Sasha wove her fingers together with Max's, the physical contact sending a prickle down her arm. Her heart beat a little faster, and her dragon released a tiny gasp. Luckily, it wasn't loud enough for Max to look askance at her. "Where are we going first?" she asked to distract herself from Max's touch.

"Let's go to the bookstore." He sent her a grin. "You can purchase more kissing books."

Heat collected in her cheeks, and it seeped down to her upper chest and breasts.

"*I want to breathe fire,*" her dragon said. "*To release the banked heat inside me.*"

"*No,*" Sasha ordered. "*That would out us. Take a deep breath.*"

"*It hasn't helped.*"

"*Keep taking deep breaths until you feel calm. We are in a town, which is full of humans. Deep breaths.*"

"*Huh,*" her dragon said. "*Wouldn't it be easier to kiss Max and get rid of the heat that way?*"

"*No! We can't do that either. It will make the heat worse. Besides, there are humans everywhere. Remember what we learned from the kissing books? Humans do that stuff in private.*"

"*Dragons do too. Mostly.*"

"*Exactly.*"

"Here is the bookstore," Max said, and he released her hand to open the door and usher her and Noel inside. "Noel, you can choose one book to take home, but first, we'll buy something for you to give Tiffany at her party."

"Dragons," Noel said.

Max laughed. "Let me ask the man at the counter if he has any children's books featuring dragons."

"Wow," Sasha whispered.

"*I've never seen so many books,*" her dragon agreed. "*Can we buy a kissing book? We've finished all the ones at Max's house.*"

"*We don't have any human money,*" Sasha said.

The owner of the bookstore showed them the children's section and pointed out several books featuring dragons, then left them alone.

"Did you find Mum's e-reader?" Max asked.

"I don't know what an e-reader is," Sasha said.

"I'm sure I saw it in the junk drawer in the kitchen," Max said. "Remind me to look for it when we get home. Mum was a prodigious reader." He winked at her. "She loved spicy kissing books."

Sasha lifted her chin. "What about the birthday gift?"

"We'll discuss these kissing books later," Max murmured.

In the end, they settled on a coloring book and a box of coloring pencils for Tiffany while they purchased a book on dragon tales for Noel.

"A kite?" Noel asked.

"Lucky for you, I know how to make one," Max said. "Dad helped me to construct a kite when I was ten. We'll make one tomorrow."

Dinner at the restaurant was a novel experience for Sasha. By watching everyone else, she thought she coped well, and Sasha enjoyed the fish and chips, a dish she'd never tried before.

"What was your favorite thing you did this week, Noel?" Max asked as they ate an ice cream sundae for dessert.

"Swimming," Noel said. "In the pool and at the beach. I practice a lot."

"You do," Sasha said.

"Thank you," Max mouthed.

Max paid for their meal, and they walked through the village to get to the castle grounds. Sasha noticed other families ambling in the same direction.

"Do lots of people visit the castle?" she asked.

"During the summer, when the evenings are still light. Let me buy an admission ticket for us. Wait here with Sasha," Max said to Noel.

It didn't take long before Max was back with their tickets. They wandered around the gardens, and Sasha enjoyed herself immensely identifying the different flowers and bushes.

"You like gardens and plants," Max said.

Noel ran from flower to flower in front of them while they observed him.

"Yes, I enjoy gardening," Sasha said. "I've learned everything I know from my grandmother."

"My grandmother loved nothing more than to get out into the garden and feel the dirt between her fingers. She grew the most amazing vegetables."

"I found the vegetable plot. Noel and I cleared it and planted seeds. He told me he used to help and seemed proficient. He knew where to find the tools and where your mother kept her seeds."

Max grasped her hand and turned her so he could study her face. She blinked, uncertain of what he wanted or what he saw when he examined her so intently.

"You are the most amazing, interesting, and mature-for-your-age woman I have ever met, yet you have a playful, passionate side, too. And you're curious about everything."

Sasha nibbled her bottom lip while her dragon remained uncharacteristically silent. Sasha swallowed. "Ah, is that bad?"

"No! Hell, Sasha, you're amazing. How old did you say you were?"

"Twenty-one."

"How is it that another man hasn't snapped you up? You're gorgeous, a hard worker. You're sincere. Hell, I told myself I wouldn't do this, but you're like an itch I can't get rid of. Our kiss before wasn't enough."

"Did he just insult us?" her dragon asked. *"We're not an itch. That sounds rude."*

"Remember when Blaze told us men are stupid?"

"Oh! He's having a manly moment," her dragon said.

"Yes."

"He's going to kiss us again," her dragon said with excitement. *"Pucker up."*

"Shush," Sasha muttered. *"I need to focus."*

Max drew her closer, took a second to make sure Noel was okay and kissed her without hesitation. He embraced her and rested his hands on her butt while his lips caressed and teased hers.

"Is it okay to do this in public?" her dragon murmured once Max had parted their lips and was nuzzling Sash's jaw and her throat. *"Ooh, that feels amazing. Should we have tried this with Bruceous? Maybe it might have changed our mind about a betrothal?"*

"No! No, no, no!" Sasha sent forcibly down their communication

link. *"Bruceous is a dirty old dragon who pinches young women on the bottom. You know, there was a rumor about him having a mistress. I bet it's true."*

"Max? Is that you, Max?" a woman asked from behind Sasha.

Max tensed a fraction before loosening his grip on Sasha and turning to face the new arrival.

The woman was beautiful, with long blonde hair that fell in a tangle of curls around her shoulders. She was slim and wore a dress that came to her mid-thigh teamed with leather sandals with a low heel. Right now, her blue eyes held pain, and after a glance at their entwined fingers, she averted her gaze to focus on Max.

"Jennifer," he said. "How are you?"

"I was wondering why I hadn't heard from you," the blonde woman said. "I thought it was because you had a lot going on with caring for your brother and starting a new job nearer to your home."

Sasha frowned at the underlying hurt in the woman's voice, the same pain she'd shown on seeing the physical contact between Sasha and Max, and studied her more closely.

"An ex-girlfriend?" her dragon asked.

Sasha didn't reply since she was concentrating on forcing down the wave of jealousy wafting from her dragon. The truth was she suffered from the same sense of envy and had to work hard to suppress it.

"Jennifer, I rang and left a message with your father when

you were unavailable," Max said in an even tone. "I explained to him about Noel and needing to care for my brother. Your father promised to pass on my message."

"He didn't," Jennifer said, her tone a trifle bitter. "Now I understand you're engaged. That was quick work."

"How did you—"

"Your grandmother belongs to the same Women's Institute group as my mother. I thought I'd investigate myself and go for a walk to sort out what I would say to you first. I was thinking about you, and suddenly there you were." Jennifer seemed to have gained in confidence, and she raked Sasha with a stern glare. "Isn't she a bit young for you?"

Sasha decided to bail Max out. She thrust out her hand and waited for Jennifer's manners to kick in. "Hi, I'm Sasha. I'm sorry you're upset, but I've known Max for a while. We argued during our last meeting, but I decided I was stupid. We've been in constant contact for some time and realized that we're better together than apart. I might look younger, but Max isn't much older than me. My mother always said I had a wise head on young shoulders. We have a lot in common. For instance, we both adore Noel." Sasha shot her a direct look when Jennifer failed to accept the handshake of peace. Sasha let her hand drop to her side. "I get the feeling your father failed to pass on Max's message because he wants nothing to do with a child who some consider imperfect?"

Heat seeped into Jennifer's cheeks. "He was wrong to withhold the message, and I apologize for his attitude. I should've contacted you earlier, Max, instead of listening to my girlfriends and giving you space. You're a wonderful man." She turned to Sasha. "Congratulations on your engagement. I hope you'll both be happy."

"Let me give you a few moments alone," Sasha said. "Noel has questions about the fish pond he's peering into so intently." Sasha forced her legs to move in Noel's direction.

"Why are we leaving them alone?" her dragon protested. *"She might win him back."*

"No, she won't. Her father's cruelty is unforgivable in Max's eyes. Max loves Noel, and he's changed his entire life to keep Noel with him. That's part of the reason Max likes us so much. Because we care for Noel as much as he does."

"And because we're gorgeous," her dragon said with a haughty sniff.

"And because we're smart and beautiful," Sasha said with a grin.

"Shasha," Noel said. "Can we have a pond with fish?"

"They're not very nutritious," her dragon said, full of doubt. *"A tiny mouthful and bones that get hooked in my teeth. They're not much better than fish fingers. Wait!"* She climbed up Sasha's neck and onto her jaw so she got an excellent view of the orange fish. *"Do those fish have hands and fingers? Aw! They don't."*

"Remember that people make fish fingers," Sasha said. *"Fish don't have hands."*

"Well, I don't get why they call them fish fingers. It makes little sense."

"We'll ask Max, but we have enough responsibility." Sasha smiled at Noel. "Remember, we're making a special garden to attract the bees and the butterflies. I'm sure Max will bring us back here again to visit the fish. It's nice for every garden to have a point of difference. Ours will have pretty butterflies and bees to make our vegetables grow. This garden has fish."

A hand crept around her waist. Its presence didn't surprise Sasha since she'd detected Max's scent.

"Is Jennifer okay?" Sasha asked. "I wanted to be jealous, but I decided you were kissing me rather than her."

"Jennifer and I went out on two dates not long after I moved back home from London. When she didn't return my call, I assumed she wasn't interested." Max shook his head and showed his white teeth in a dazzling grin. "Most women would shout or cross-examine me. You stuck up for me, then you tell me you're jealous. You are one in a million, Sasha. The more time I spend with you, the more I like you. And thank you for explaining to Noel about the fish. You handled him beautifully."

"Can we go to the puzzle?" Noel asked.

"What's that?" Sasha asked.

"It's a labyrinth. The castle has a maze too, but Noel doesn't like that as much. He became separated from Mum and Dad one time, and it took a while to find him," Max said.

"What is the difference between the two?" Sasha asked, not knowing what either item was but not wanting to appear stupid. Soon, Max would wonder why she didn't understand things most humans took for granted. So far, with the help of Justine, The Smart Computer, she'd muddled her way through most subjects.

"A maze is a lot of plants that grow together. There are paths with some dead-ends. The object is to find your way to the center of the maze. They build a labyrinth in the same manner, but the plants are usually ankle-height, and there are no dead-ends. They're a popular meditation tool since it is very restful to walk around one."

Sasha enjoyed exploring and walking the labyrinth with Noel and Max. She was sorry when it was time for them to go home, but Noel was visibly drooping. He'd undoubtedly sleep well tonight. Max picked up his brother and carried Noel on his shoulders back to the car. Noel fell asleep during the drive home.

"Thank you for taking us out," Sasha said. "I enjoyed it immensely."

"I wish we could fly," Sasha's dragon said. *"It's a beautiful night."*

The second her dragon suggested a flight, Sasha felt twitchy in her skin. They were used to flying whenever they felt like it, and this enforced separation from her other self seemed unnecessarily restrictive, even if it was for their safety.

"We'll see," Sasha said. *"We must act with caution. You've seen what they do to their people with the weapons they call guns."*

Her dragon snorted. *"Justine, The Smart Computer, told us those are fictional games we were watching."*

"We will ask her more about actual wars tomorrow," Sasha said. *"To gain a balanced opinion."*

"Very well."

On arrival home, Max carried Noel inside and up to his bedroom. His phone rang, and he pulled it from his pocket to scowl at the screen. "I have to take this," he said, his voice holding impatience. "Hello."

"No problem. I'll get Noel ready for bed," Sasha said, having heard the arrogant voice at the other end of the conversation.

"I wonder who that was?" her dragon asked, thankfully distracted from a night flight.

"Hang on, boss. Let me get my notes."

Max left the bedroom, and Sasha listened for as long as she could. Thankfully, a dragon's hearing was excellent. *"He sounds like a nasty man."*

"Bruceous's cousin," her dragon agreed.

Sasha helped Noel change into pajamas, and he was so tired he fell asleep immediately. Sasha walked down to the kitchen to make a cup of hot chocolate—a new favorite—and Max appeared as she pulled a mug from the cupboard.

"Is Noel okay?"

"He's asleep," she said. "We tired him out."

"I was hoping to have a few days at home, but I need to take care of several interviews and write a story about the dragon people saw two weeks ago. Then, I have to head back to Edinburgh because my boss has a new story for me that requires my presence at the office. In these days of digital, I don't understand why he can't do this online."

"It doesn't matter," Sasha said. "I'm here, and Noel and I are perfectly happy."

"But my grandmother argues I'm always working and therefore I can't look after Noel properly. Having to return to Edinburgh all the time is proving her point."

"Have you talked to your boss?"

"He told me he understood and working from home wouldn't be a problem when I attended the job interview. He seems to have done a three-sixty."

"How did you get the job?"

"I applied after I saw it in the local paper."

Sasha stilled, a thought occurring. Several times during outings with Noel, she'd sensed someone watching them. Even tonight, although that could've been the woman, Jennifer. "Does your boss know your grandmother or your grandfather?"

Max stared at her, his mouth agape. "I didn't think of that, but surely my grandmother wouldn't go that far to win custody of Noel?"

CHAPTER 7

A Bully and a Bribe

Max plonked his butt on the nearest chair and stared at Sasha. His grandmother couldn't be so callous. He hated to harbor these suspicions of her, yet now that Sasha had mentioned it, his mind refused to leave the topic alone.

Sasha set a mug of hot chocolate in front of him.

"Thanks," he said absently. "Mum and Dad left a large trust fund for Noel's benefit. They explained it to me before they died and told me I had more advantages than Noel. This was their way of evening the stakes." He lifted his gaze to Sasha's concerned face. "Whoever has Noel living with them has access to the trust. All they need to do is present the relevant invoices to the lawyers who oversee the trust." He shook his head. "No, I can't believe that of my grandparents."

"Money does strange things to people," Sasha said. "Perhaps you should check it out with the lawyers and learn what type of invoices your grandparents are submitting for payment. Can you do that?"

"I'll contact the lawyers tomorrow," Max said. "Which reminds me. You need to ask for receipts and keep a record of items you buy for Noel."

"I used the money you left to buy coffee for me and a drink for Noel. We'll go on the bus this week."

"Mum used to have bus passes," Max said. "I'll look for them later and leave them out for you. I'm sorry tonight ended on such a bum note."

"It's not your fault if you have to work."

"If my grandmother is plotting, then I must bear part of the blame." Max ruffled his hair, and his chest lifted in a hearty sigh. When had his life run so far out of control? He felt as if he was on a runaway train with his jurisdiction over everything important, crumbling with each new revelation. Sasha was right, though. Now that the suspicions had raised their ugly heads, he had to investigate.

Sasha reached across the table for his hand. "You're judging yourself too harshly. We should be able to trust our family."

Max grimaced. "Instead of these heavy thoughts, I'd intended to flirt with you. Kiss you again. And ask more questions about the kissing books you've been reading." His tone turned teasing. "When I'm searching for the bus tickets, I'll keep an eye out for Mum's e-reader."

"Thank you. I find the books diverse here. More interesting."

Curiosity rose in him for the *nth* time. Sasha didn't speak much of her life before coming here, merely dropping a hint here and there. "Are your parents strict?"

"With me—yes. It's because I'm the youngest of four and the only girl. My parents insist on knowing where I'm going and who I'm seeing."

"How did you get permission to come to the UK?"

"It's a long and complicated story." Sasha didn't avoid his gaze, yet the lift of her chin told him that was all she intended to say on the matter.

"Have you argued with your parents?"

Sasha hesitated. "Not exactly, but they want me to marry a family friend."

Max stared, almost shocked by her revelation. "Is that why you left home?"

"I was angry when I left," Sasha conceded, and it was apparent she measured her words. "This man is much older than me, and I don't believe we have much in common."

"Tell your parents no and explain why you and this man wouldn't suit," Max said. "Would they approve of me?"

Sasha grinned, the blast of humor taking her face from beautiful to stunning. Those gorgeous blue eyes of hers. That brown hair with copper highlights. He saw them in his dreams. "Do parents ever approve of a daughter's suitor?"

Max grinned. "Am I a suitor?"

She wrinkled her nose, instigating an urgent need for him to breach the gap between them and claim her. Holding hands wasn't enough. "No clue. Do you want to be? Is this a proper thing, considering I'm working for you and looking after Noel?"

"It's right if you're happy with my attention. You should never feel coerced or frightened of me. All you ever need to do is say no, and the kissing ends." His heart stuttered before racing into a frenzied beat. God, the last thing he ever wanted to do was frighten her or force his attentions on her.

"As the youngest in my family, I was the annoying little sister who insisted on tagging along with her brothers. I particularly used to drive Blaze, my oldest brother, crazy by following him. I promised to follow my other brothers instead of him if he showed me how to fight. That was when one of the other dr...kids tried to bully me. Let's just say that Blaze did a stellar job, and I'm more than capable of looking after myself. If I hated your kisses, you'd know about it."

Relief filled Max at her words. Once again, she met his gaze without hesitation. She radiated honesty and integrity.

"I need to leave early to get to the office on time. I'd better go to bed and grab a bit of sleep." It was the last thing he wanted to do, but he stood and strode to the kitchen drawer where his mother had kept a selection of bits and bobs. As he suspected, the bus passes were there. Three of them. He pulled out Noel's pass plus his mother's and handed them to Sasha. "The bus passes. I haven't used a bus for ages, so I'm not sure what you do. The driver will let you know."

"I can ask Justine, The Smart Computer," Sasha said.

"Ah! The e-reader is here. It will probably require charging. Great. Here's the charger." He handed both over to her, hesitating because he wanted to kiss her again.

She grinned at him without warning. "Do I get a goodnight kiss?"

"Yes," he said, reaching her side in one colossal stride. He held her close, content to cuddle at first. She sank against his chest, apparently happy with the physical contact too. After a long moment, he drew back and grinned down at her. "You're amazing, Sasha."

A beat later, he was kissing her, savoring her quick intake of breath and her shy return of the caress. She licked his lower lip and nipped it lightly. Heat, pleasure, and a desire for more surged through him, but he kept the kiss light so as not to test his willpower.

He withdrew a few seconds later, placed a kiss on her forehead, and stepped back. "Thank you for looking after Noel. I'll call you every night, and hopefully, I'll be home at the weekend."

Max forced himself to walk away from Sasha. It was more challenging than he'd assumed, and it told him he was as attached to Sasha as Noel. When she was here, they worked as a team. Although he loved his younger brother, there had been the odd time when he'd resented having to return to Bamburgh. He'd wanted his independence again, but Sasha had soothed the restlessness in him with her smart and sassy personality.

He believed her when she told him she could look after herself. Max smiled, recalling her expression when she'd mentioned the man her parents wanted her to marry. She loathed the man. Lucky for him. He wondered if her parents would approve of him. Too bad, because he was awfully tempted to make their fake engagement into a real one. Sasha intrigued him, and every bit of information he uncovered about her only drove him to want more.

Yep, it seemed he wanted a woman.

Sasha.

The next week passed faster than Sasha liked because it meant the days were ticking by, and she wasn't attempting to return home. Oh, it was easy enough for her and her dragon to understand the why.

One: she relished looking after Noel, and each day was a new adventure. She and Noel were learning lots of astounding things every day.

Two: the more she learned about Max and the more she chatted with him, the more she liked the sexy man.

Three: if she returned home now, her parents would force her to marry Bruceous. Of that, she had little doubt.

And four: each time she and Noel walked outside, she sensed someone was watching them. Following them. So far, she hadn't glimpsed the person, but they'd soon slip. She'd ignored the intrusion while keeping a close eye on Noel.

But as the days passed, guilt battered her because her parents would be worried—her brothers. At first, her parents would've been angry because they'd think she'd disobeyed them. Now, they'd have reached the concerned stage.

"To be fair," her dragon said, *"We have visited the beach most days. We can sense the barrier, which means there is no way to return to Perfume Isle."*

"True."

"Can we read the latest kissing book now?"

"As soon as we drop Noel off at kindergarten," Sasha promised. *"We need to mop the floor and clean the kitchen, but I'm certain we can fit in some reading."*

"Are you ready to leave, Noel?" Sasha said.

"Don't wanna go." Noel folded his arms, and he hunched inward.

Surprise filled Sasha. Noel was such a cheerful kid, and he loved playing with the other children. "Why not?"

"Don't like Darren. He's mean." Noel's eyes turned glossy, and a tear slipped free.

"A bully," her dragon said. *"We can fix that if we shift to a dragon and scare him."*

"We can't threaten a child. Think of a way to fix it while we're in our human form. There's no reason why we can't let you show through my eyes when we're speaking with Darren and his mother."

"Ooh, plan. I get to be a baddie. I like it."

"Noel, would it help if I stayed at kindergarten with you for a while? We'll talk to the teacher or Darren's mother if the teacher can't help."

Noel's doubt slid across his round face and settled into a huge frown. "Not going."

Sasha crouched in front of him and placed her hands on his thin shoulders. "Sometimes, we have to do things we don't want to do. It helps us when we grow older and teaches us a life lesson. Did you know my mother told me that?"

"Yeah, when she first introduced the idea of Bruceous for our husband. Blah!" Her dragon did a barfing sound that made Sasha want to giggle.

"Shush, we have to concentrate on Noel right now."

"Tell him he'll disappoint Max."

"You know how hard Max works?" she asked Noel.

He didn't react, but his gaze tracked to her face and remained. "Max wanted to live and work in London, but he changed his life around so he could look after you and spend time with you. Max has to work to pay for things like kindergarten." Did he understand? "If Max didn't go to work, you wouldn't have nice food and trips to the castle. You wouldn't have books and coloring pencils or crayons."

"That's not working. Bribe the kid," her dragon said.

Agreeing, Sasha tried a new tack. "If you go to kindergarten today, I will do my best to make Darren stop being mean to you, and we'll do something special this afternoon. How does that sound? A surprise."

Noel brightened. "Surprise now."

"No," Sasha stated. "If I let you stay home today instead of going to kindergarten, you don't get a surprise. Instead, we'll do jobs, and I'm afraid I'll have to punish you. No beach visits, either."

Noel stamped his foot. "Not fair. Want surprise."

"Those are the Sasha rules," Sasha said, speaking in a stern voice when she wanted to give him a quick cuddle and fight his battles for him. It wouldn't help him, and she sensed Max would agree with her. "How about this? It's kindergarten this morning, and I'll help you with meanie Darren. If this doesn't work, we'll bring in the big guns and consult with Max."

"Want surprise."

"Only if you go to kindergarten," Sasha countered calmly.

Noel stared at her, his cheeks turning pink. Sasha returned his intense gaze, wryly thinking she'd stepped into her mother's shoes. Instead of agreeing with Sasha, Noel finally stomped to the bag he took with him to kindergarten and picked it up.

"Want surprise," he stated.

"When we get home from kindergarten," Sasha promised.

Noel didn't say much during their walk to kindergarten, which was unusual because he'd become quite a chatterbox.

"We'd better have an excellent surprise ready for him. He resembles a martyr from our storybooks," her dragon said.

"Which one is Darren?"

Noel pointed out a kid with red hair and freckles. He wasn't larger than Noel, but when Sasha spotted him, he was pushing a little girl.

"Right, that does it," her dragon snapped. *"Let's break his twig arms."*

"Steady, this requires diplomacy with a bit of dragon to back up our claims." She gathered herself and smiled encouragement at Noel. "Noel, wait there."

Sasha strode over to Darren and his current victim. She'd almost reached him when he pushed the girl again, and this time she fell. Sasha scooped her up and placed her on her feet before turning her attention to Darren. She crouched to his height and stared him in the face. Aware of her limited time, Sasha let her dragon appear in her eyes and voice. "I saw what you just did," she rumbled. "That was mean, Darren, and if you continue with this behavior, I will visit your house. You don't want that. Stop pushing little girls and stop being mean to Noel or else," she added in a threatening tone.

"Grrrrr," her dragon added.

The color departed from Darren's cheeks, leaving his ginger freckles standing out like a map of crazy dots. Having done the best she could, Sasha stood and turned to check on the little girl. Noel had his arm around her shoulders, and they were studying the blood dripping down her knee.

A smile curved her mouth, and pride swelled within her.

"Aw, that is so sweet," her dragon cooed.

"Is Carly all right?" the teacher asked.

"We need some blood clean-up," Sasha said. "Darren gave her a fright pushing her that way. He's been bullying Noel too. Noel didn't want to come to kindergarten this morning."

The teacher's mouth firmed as she sent a glare of disapproval in Darren's direction. "Thank you for telling me. I've had reports from other parents, and they've complained about his bullying. I'll call his mother now and get her to pick him up."

"Thank you," Sasha said. "It concerned me when Noel refused to come because he usually loves his mornings here."

"No, I appreciate your comments. We prefer to stomp out bad behavior as soon as possible."

Sasha had almost reached Max's house when she sensed someone watching her again. This time, when she walked to the front door, she caught a scent.

"*It stops at the door,*" her dragon said.

"*Yes. It's not the mail lady because we know her perfume.*"

"*Perhaps it was one of those selling people that knock on your door. We read about them in* Passion with the Salesman.*"

"*Possibly, but we're not letting them in if they return,*" Sasha said. "*I'd prefer to kiss Max.*"

"*Agreed,*" her dragon said immediately.

"*Well, they're not here now. We'll catalog their scent, and if they come again, we'll recognize them.*"

"*You promised Noel a surprise. What will you do?*"

"*I thought we'd make a simple labyrinth on the lawn. Max said it needed mowing.*"

"*Ooh, we get to use the machine. Max told us to wait.*"

"*But he showed us how to start it when we asked. I thought we could map out a simple labyrinth and mow the lawn for the path. That way, we can alter the pattern once we get sick of the first one. Noel enjoyed the design the other night.*"

"*Can we do that?*"

"*Sure,*" Sasha said. "*We'll ask Justine, The Smart Computer. She'll help us.*"

And she did. By the time it was time to collect Noel, they had a basic spiral labyrinth on the back lawn.

"Where is the surprise?" Noel asked the second he saw Sasha.

"That's not very polite, young man. You should say hello first."

"Hello, Shasha. Where is my surprise?"

She chortled and chucked him under the chin. "It's at home. It was too big to pack inside my bag."

His eyebrows lifted. "What is it?"

Sasha tapped her nose. "Surprise."

As they opened the front gate, Sasha paused. The same scent was here again and more potent as if the person had visited for a second time.

Her dragon tattoo climbed high on her neck. *"I can't see anyone, but they've walked through the gate to the house. Can't hear anything. The birds are singing."*

Sasha opened the gate and ushered Noel through. "What would you like for lunch? Sandwiches again?"

"Yes, please," Noel said. "I'm hungry."

"You didn't tell me how your morning went. Did Darren stay, or did his mother pick him up?"

"Darren left with his mother. She was shouting at him."

"I see," Sasha said. "That's what happens when you're mean-spirited."

"Mean-spirited," Noel parroted.

Sasha paused, her hand on the front door. The stranger had stood right here—she could smell him. His scent covered the wood as if he'd tried to push the door. The weight of a stare at her back told her the man or someone else was watching again.

"I'm tired of this," her dragon said. *"I wish they'd show themselves so we could go* Buffy *on their butts. We need to find one of those wooden stake things. Where do you buy those? Will Justine, The Smart Computer, know?"*

"I think stakes only work for vampires. We'd need to see this watcher's teeth first." Sasha unlocked the door and ushered Noel inside.

"Is my surprise here?"

"No," Sasha said. "We'll have a drink and a sandwich first, then I'll show you your surprise. I suspect you'll want to play with it for a while before you have your nap."

"Don't want a nap," Noel said in his usual protest.

"Remember the Sasha rules. No nap. No beach."

He frowned, his nose wrinkling.

"We have the same discussion every day," her dragon complained.

"He's no different from us when we were his age," Sasha said. *"Remember?"*

"Oh. Yeah. We still tell our mother no."

"The difference being that we're no longer a child."

"We are in dragon years," her dragon pointed out.

"True, but we're not on Perfume Isle at present, so the rules don't apply. I hate the thought of worrying our parents and brothers, but I love the freedom we have to make our own decisions."

Sasha made a cheese and pickle sandwich for Noel and another for herself.

"What did you do at kindy today?"

"Teacher told story about mean boy and girl. Didn't like them."

"I see. Did you draw pictures today?"

"Painting with fingers," Noel said. "Wore smocks over clothes. Used fingers."

"That sounds like fun, and it also explains the red and the purple paint under your fingernails, young man."

Noel giggled, and Sasha smiled.

"Surprise?" Noel asked.

She tweaked Noel's nose. "You have a one-track mind, mister. Okay. Let me clear the table and put everything away."

Five minutes later, Sasha steered Noel outside. "I made you a labyrinth," she said. "It's different from the one at the castle. Do you like it?"

When Noel didn't comment, she said, "Let me show you how it works."

Sasha took his hand and led him to the starting point. "The short grass is the path, and the long is the boundary. Do you see?"

He clapped his hands in clear approval and started ambling, using the same focus he had the previous night when walking the labyrinth with Max.

"It's a win," her dragon said. *"He still limps, but he seems stronger from the daily exercise."*

"A huge win," Sasha agreed. *"Do you sense the spy?"*

"Yes," her dragon replied, her tone unhappy. *"If we didn't have to guard Noel, I'd confront the man and tell him to go away."*

"We'll keep watching, but we'll fool him. I'll face Noel and keep an eye on him while you resettle and spy above my collar."

"Plan," her dragon said and resituated herself on Sasha's back.

"Can you see anyone?"

"Not clearly. He's hiding behind a bush and is inspecting us through one of those camera things."

"All right. We'll check him out once Noel is having his nap. We'll pretend to work in the garden and sneak up on him."

"That will be easy. All we need to do is follow his smell. It's obvious he has no close acquaintance with soap."

Noel walked the labyrinth three times, and Sasha strolled with him.

"Do you like your surprise?"

"Yes." He beamed at her. "Walk again."

"One more before you go for your nap. I thought I might teach you a new swimming thing at the beach. Would you like that?"

"Yes!"

"If the sun goes away, we'll collect driftwood and shells instead. We can make a picture out of them."

"Okay," Noel said.

"That was easy," her dragon said.

"He enjoys doing new things. Although it takes him a while to learn to do something, he gets bored if we repeat an activity too many

times in a row."

After Noel's nap, the journey to the beach was slow because they came across a plant covered with ladybirds.

"*Someone is still observing us,*" Sasha said. "*I haven't spotted them, which is most frustrating.*"

Her dragon issued a testy growl. "*I can't see them either.*"

"*Well, they'll slip up, eventually.*"

"*What will we do when we catch them?*"

"*It depends on their purpose.*"

Her dragon sniffed. "*If our gorgeous form attracts them, they should come out of hiding and speak to us.*"

Sasha bit back a grin. "*I like Max.*"

"*I like Max too, which is why anyone else can look but not touch.*"

Sasha cackled aloud at that one.

"Why are you laughing?" Noel asked.

"Because I'm happy. I don't think we'll swim today since it's cooler, but we can paddle. And we can make a sandcastle or collect shells and driftwood."

"You turn into a dragon today?" Noel asked.

Sasha stilled.

"*Luckily, no one believes him,*" her dragon said.

"Not today," Sasha replied. "My dragon is sleepy."

"*Hey, if we get a fat arse from lack of exercise, it will be your fault,*" her dragon snapped. "*Although there was that kissing book where the man liked junk in the trunk.*"

Sasha had enjoyed that romance since the man had loved the woman and hadn't tried to change her. *"I bet Bruceous would try to mold us to what he wants."*

"Another reason we should stay here. Give the dirty old dragon a chance to focus on another unfortunate debutante."

When they reached the beach, Sasha kicked off her sandals. "Shall we leave our towels and shoes in a pile and go for a walk? Let's see how many crabs we can spot today. I bet we will see nine. How many do you guess?"

"Six," Noel said instantly. His favorite number. He tugged at his sandals and set them beside Sasha's in a nice straight line.

"All right. If I win, you have to help me make dinner." Sasha bit her lip, so she didn't laugh again. Noel loved cooking and helped her every night.

Noel bobbed his head in enthusiasm, and she held out her hand for him. His stubby fingers clasped hers, and they set off to investigate the shoreline.

Sasha paddled in the shallow water, but Noel released her hand and ran ahead to peer into the many tiny holes.

"One," he shouted and trotted farther along the sand.

Sasha let him run ahead but kept watch. She couldn't see any other people on the beach today, the dull weather driving everyone indoors.

"There's a running man," her dragon said. *"Why do humans enjoy running so much? Why doesn't he have proper stylish clothes if*

he's racing so fast? Humans seem to like their stretching clothes that show off their fat rolls."

"Now that is plain bitchy," Sasha chided.

The man raced past her and headed straight for Noel.

"Can't he see Noel?" her dragon asked as Sasha stiffened in alarm. *"Stupid man. He's got the entire beach to run on, and he sprints on a collision path with a child. Dragons are not that dumb."*

"Hey!" Sasha shouted.

The man didn't stop. If anything, he increased his speed, still heading straight for Noel. An instant later, he seized Noel and continued running, carrying the boy under his arm like an ungainly parcel.

"Hey!" Sasha yelled and started in pursuit.

"I hate running," her dragon snapped.

Sasha increased her speed.

"Shift," her dragon shouted at her. *"Let me breathe fire at his legs."*

"No, you might hurt Noel," Sasha gasped.

The man was increasing his lead, despite Noel's kicking and shouting.

"Shift! Otherwise, we won't catch him."

"Okay," Sasha puffed, accepting that her dragon could move so much faster than her. She slowed and struggled out of her clothes. Before she'd yanked her T-shirt over her head, her shift burst through her. Painfully fast, her body expanded, and scales rippled over her skin. Seconds later, she was airborne, and not a moment too soon.

From above, it was easy to see the man abducting Noel was heading for the car park, and he had an accomplice waiting with the engine of his car engaged.

Sasha's dragon flapped her wings extra hard, her sleek form arrowing toward the kidnapper. She roared her fury and flew past the man carrying Noel. Her gaze on Noel, she inserted herself between the car and the man and hovered. He was still wriggling and screeching and making it difficult for the man to maintain hold of him.

"Give him a reason to drop Noel," Sasha ordered her dragon.

In response, her dragon blasted the ground with a wall of flames. The man came to a screeching halt.

"Shasha!" Noel screamed. "Shasha."

The man didn't release Noel but froze, gawking at her. An instant later, he seemed to shake from his stupor, darted around the fire and scampered for the waiting vehicle.

Her dragon bugled her fury, and the next second, she fired at the car. Flames danced across the car's roof. The man waiting in the driver's seat leaped out and ran for cover.

Sasha focused on the man still gripping Noel. Her dragon dive-bombed the man. Obviously sensing he couldn't escape—not if he tried to take Noel with him—he dropped Noel.

Noel let out a yelp, but Sasha didn't hesitate. Her dragon

swooped down and grabbed Noel in her talon. Seconds later, she was darting along the beach, keeping low as she sped over the sand to where they'd left their clothes.

"We'll fly home," her dragon announced.

"No, we've already risked too much. We don't want too many humans to spot us."

"But what if the men ambush us? We'll fly." Her dragon's tone suggested that no matter what argument Sasha mounted, she'd lose.

Sasha bit her tongue and prayed a limited number of people spotted their overhead flight and their landing in Max's backyard. At least the weather was acting in their favor, the lack of sunshine and promise of rain driving people indoors. But still... Her gut bucked and roiled, and she tried to watch the passing blur of scenery. At least her dragon was putting on a burst of speed instead of taking a leisurely circle of Bamburgh.

"How is Noel?"

"Not sure," her dragon said. "He's not crying, and he's not struggling."

"Poor kid is in shock."

"Well, what should we have done?" her dragon snapped. "Those men were trying to steal him. If we'd let them, Max would've sacked us in the same way the woman in the kissing book lost her job."

"Max would never blame us," Sasha said. "We chased after the thief and almost caught him."

"He was going to get away. He might have hurt Noel. Horrible things happen here. You've seen the news on the telly."

"Is our world any better?" Sasha asked. Their parents and brothers loved and protected them, but most dragons gave humans little respect. The older dragons held grudges. Some resented their new cage and wished to return to the world on the mainland.

"Most of the dragons wouldn't survive here," her dragon said. *"Not with the weapons, the planes, and guns we've seen on television. Remember the pictures and the stories Justine showed us about the wars the humans have fought since our kind retreated to Dragon Isles. We can't compete with the human's machine guns and bombs. In a war between the species, the humans would win."*

"Which is why I didn't want to reveal our dragon," Sasha said in a tight voice.

"Too late. We're at the house."

Sasha groaned as she spotted the startled faces of a man and a woman out walking their dog. This was one big cluster, and she'd bet her grandmother's emerald bracelet that these weren't the only people who'd spotted them this afternoon.

CHAPTER 8

Go Get That Dragon

"**M**ax!"

Max heard his boss's holler from two offices away. With a sigh, he pushed up from his office chair and trudged toward the roar that resembled a mythical dragon.

"News is coming in," his boss shouted, excitement making him bounce like a child. "Several people have spotted a dragon flying near Bamburgh Castle."

"What color?" Max asked deadpan.

"Bronze," his boss replied without missing a beat. "Get me the story."

Max gaped at him. *A dragon.* He shook his head, waiting for the joke's punchline.

"Why are you standing there? Bring me the scoop. My contacts are credible."

"Are you sure they haven't been drinking?"

"Max!" his boss roared. "Get the damn story. Remember, you got this job as a family favor. I can, however, sack you as quick as I hired you."

"Pardon?" Max asked.

"Why are you still here? *Dragon*. Huge, huge story. Tremendous story."

Max strode away, his mind working busily. He'd applied for this job after seeing it in the local paper. At the time, a job near home had been a godsend when Noel had needed him. But now, he wondered if his grandmother *had* manipulated him from behind the scenes.

Max wheeled around and stalked back to his boss's office. "Which family favor got me this job?"

His boss stilled. "Let me make this clear. If I see you in this office again today, I will fire you, and then what will you do for money?"

Although he hadn't answered, Max had enough information to make a calculated guess. Manipulated him. No wonder his boss had summoned him back to work early and thank every god for Sasha's strength and integrity. He couldn't have a better person to look after Noel when he couldn't be there to do it himself. If his assumptions were right, then his grandmother had looked at

Sasha's youth and thought to manipulate her. She'd failed once, but his grandmother had another plan up her sleeve if she'd had him recalled to Edinburgh.

Max speared one harsh glare at his boss and turned on his heel. He stopped by his office and cleared his desk. It was time for him to take a stand against the hidden enemy. Actually, not so hidden since his grandmother's fingers were all over this manipulation. He'd do some other job, and his boss could suck eggs. Ten minutes later, he walked out of the newspaper office, determined never to return.

"Hey, Max. Wait up!"

Max glanced over his shoulder and hid his grimace.

"Wait up! The boss wants me to go with you to take photos. Says it's the biggest story to hit for months, and we aren't about to miss out on our big payday," the paper photographer called. The portion of his face visible above his beard had turned red, and he was breathing hard. Wisps of hair had escaped his ponytail and surrounded his face like a halo.

Max grunted. "I'm going home."

"Please, Max. I need this job. If I get the sack, I won't make my mortgage payment for this month. My wife and I are already working every hour we can. Please."

Max sighed. He couldn't kick a man who was only trying to do his job and survive. "I'm not coming back to Edinburgh."

"No problem," the photographer said. "I'll email my photos and head home using the train or a bus. Don't care. Just give me a chance to get this dragon with my camera."

"You agree a dragon is flying around Bamburgh?" Max asked.

The photographer shrugged. "Truly, I have no clue, but the paper has two credible sources. At least, that's what the boss told me."

During the drive to Bamburgh, the photographer prattled on about everything and nothing while Max wondered what the hell he'd do now.

He had to have a job to pay for household expenses. His parents had set up a trust for Noel, and the income from that trust went toward Noel's upkeep and costs. Max received the quarterly payment as Noel's current guardian, but only a portion of that went toward the household expenses.

The house cost a lot to maintain. He could downsize, but he hated to tear Noel away from an environment he loved, where he felt settled.

A dilemma.

Max lived to write innovative stories, and he wasn't doing that in Edinburgh.

"The traffic is heavy," the photographer pointed out when they came to yet another halt.

"Yes," Max said in an understatement.

His average drive time of three-quarters of an hour lengthened to over an hour before they'd even arrived at the outskirts of

Bamburgh.

"Hell," the photographer said, tugging his salt-and-pepper beard in agitation. "I recognize some of those vehicles. Every newshound in the country is chasing the dragon. Where was the sighting?"

"At the beach. I'll park at my place and walk. In this traffic, it'll be much faster."

It took them much longer to get to his house than he'd anticipated. When they arrived, vehicles surrounded his home. Two men were hammering on his front door, their determination to gain entrance underlined by the loudness of their thumps.

What the hell?

"Who are you?" Max demanded. "Why are you banging down my front door?"

The men whipped around, and Max recognized them as reporters from larger London newspapers. He'd worked with one during his time in the city.

"Max?" the man said in surprise. "You live here?"

"My parents' house," Max said in a stiff voice. "You didn't answer. Why are you thumping on the door?"

"Witnesses saw the dragon land here and enter your house," his acquaintance said.

Max's brows rose. "The dragon landed here? And entered my house? How? My home seems to be in one piece, and I doubt a dragon would fit inside without damaging the building. Now stand aside and let me enter."

The two men exchanged a glance and backed up to let Max pass. He plucked his keys from his pocket and entered. The two men attempted to follow him inside, but Max shut the door in their faces and locked the door.

"Sasha! Noel! Where are you?" He turned toward the family room since he could hear low voices.

"Max. Max. Max!" Noel hurtled from the den and flew at him, gripping Max around the knees. "Someone tried to steal me, and Shasha saved me."

"What? Where's Sasha?"

"In here, Max." Her voice sounded subdued and less Sasha than normal.

Concern zapped him. Was Noel telling the truth? Long strides took him into the room where they spent most of their time. "What's going on? Noel said someone grabbed him?"

Sasha bit her bottom lip, hesitating in a way that had his warning signals blaring.

"Tell me what happened."

"We visited the beach as we do most afternoons. Instead of swimming today, Noel and I walked and collected shells. The entire time, I suspected someone was watching us. We had almost walked to the car park halfway along the beach when I noticed a runner. Instead of continuing past us, he ran at Noel and seized him. He took off with Noel. I gave chase and caught him before he could stuff Noel in the waiting car and drive off."

"There was a waiting car?"

"Yes, the driver had the engine going."

"I don't understand. How did you grab Noel back when there were two men? Did someone help you?"

"Shasha turned into her dragon and scared the men. She blew fire, and then she picked me up, and we flew back here. It was like a book adventure," Noel shouted.

Max gaped at his brother, then glanced at Sasha and waited for her to deny everything. She didn't, merely averting her gaze and continuing to bite her lip.

"Did you call the cops?"

Sasha shook her head. "I tried to ring you, but it kept going to voicemail."

Max winced. He hadn't wanted his boss to call him for updates, so he'd turned off his phone. "I'm sorry."

Someone banged on the front door. "Max Lombardy, please come to the door. It's the police."

"At last," he muttered. "Someone to make sense out of this."

He strode to the door, unlocked it, and flung it open. Two policemen stood in the doorway. The tallest one—a man with cropped black hair and a close-trimmed black beard—handed him an envelope then paused a beat, his gaze going beyond Max to land on Sasha and Noel. Irritation flooded Max when he noted the appreciation in the policeman's eyes. The other cop, with red hair and blue eyes, maintained a professional mien. Thankfully.

"Mine," Max stated and stepped back before slamming the door. *Oh, very mature, Max,* he mocked himself, but his inner caveman hated the cop's expression. Anger pulsed through him again. The entire time he'd been away from Sasha and Noel, he'd thought about them, and the highlight of his day was the evening video calls where Noel told him the details of his morning and afternoon. His little brother was thriving under Sasha's care, despite someone trying to kidnap...

"Fuck," he ground out and flung open the door. "Can you wait?" What the hell was wrong with him? Someone had attempted to grab Noel, and he was letting his drama get in front of his brother's safety. "I want to report an attempted abduction."

The policemen paused and exchanged a glance. They retraced their steps.

"An abduction? Is that why the reporters are baying for your blood?" the red-haired cop asked.

"Me?" Max clapped a hand to his chest. "I haven't been home for long. Someone reported they saw a dragon."

The taller cop snorted in disbelief. "What have they been drinking?"

Max barked out a laugh. "That's what I said."

"You wanted to report an attempted abduction?"

"Yes," Max said. "My fiancée and my brother were taking a walk on the beach. Someone grabbed Noel and tried to shove him in a car," Max said. "It was only luck that Sasha rescued Noel."

"Can we talk to them?" the dark-haired cop asked.

The other answered a ringing mobile and spoke in low tones.

"Come in," Max said and stood aside to usher them indoors.

"Can I get you a cup of tea?" Sasha asked from the doorway of the family room.

The red-haired cop shoved his phone into his pocket. "I wish we could, but our station needs us for crowd control. We'll take your report and head back to the station."

The black-haired cop studied Sasha again, and this time Max kept his jealousy at bay. Max ushered them to the kitchen table and pulled out a seat. He gestured for the cops to take a chair. "This is my fiancée, Sasha."

"Sasha, can you tell us what happened?" the dark-haired cop asked.

"It is as Max said. Noel and I go to the beach in the afternoons. Most days, we swim, but today was a bit cooler, so we collected shells instead. We'd almost walked along as far as the car park. It's around halfway along the beach. A jogger came toward us, and I thought he was out for a run. We see runners every day. But this man veered straight for us and grabbed Noel. I raced after him shouting, but I didn't catch him until the car park. He had a friend waiting in a vehicle. The engine was running for a quick getaway. I was desperate because I knew the moment they stuffed Noel inside, they'd be off. Somehow, I grabbed the man, and Noel fell out of the car. The guy jumped into the car with his friend, and they drove off."

Noel had wandered into the kitchen and leaned against Sasha as she spoke.

"Can you give me a description of the men?" the tall cop asked.

"The one that grabbed Noel was taller than Max and skinny. He wore sunglasses and a cap. I couldn't see his hair, so it must've been short. He was wearing a faded blue T-shirt with a shape or design on the front. I don't know what it was, only that it was red lettering. He had on black shorts and running shoes."

"What about the man in the car?"

"I couldn't see much of him. He wore sunglasses too, and I got the impression he was overweight."

"Excellent," the cop said. "What about the car they were driving?"

"It was brown." She pulled a face. "I'm not good with car models. I looked at the number plate, but the numbers and letters were unreadable. Someone had covered them with mud."

"What time did this happen?"

"Around two hours ago," Sasha said.

"Why didn't you call us immediately?" the red-haired cop demanded, his eyes narrowing.

"They terrified Noel. I wasn't much better," Sasha said firmly. "It's taken us a while to calm down."

"You—" The cop broke off and took a visible breath. "Where

were you when this happened?" he asked Max.

"Edinburgh."

"Is that why you've come home?" the dark-haired cop asked.

"No, although I would've returned immediately once I'd heard about the abduction. My brother is my priority. My boss wanted me to investigate the rumors of a dragon sighting."

"I see," the red-haired cop said.

Max's mouth tightened. Hell, they both knew the dragon sighting was a load of rubbish.

The taller cop glanced at Noel and back at Max. "Can I ask Noel a few questions?"

Max shared a glance with Sasha, took in her frown but decided a few questions wouldn't hurt.

"Hello." The cop gentled his voice and smiled at Noel. "Can you tell me what happened?"

"A man picked me up," Noel said. "He ran away with me. But Shasha came. She turned into a dragon and rescued me."

A nervous giggle emerged from Sasha, one Max had never heard before from the confident woman. "I did turn into a bit of a dragon," she confessed. "I was desperate to save you."

"You breathed fire." Noel's grin was broad.

"I did," Sasha said. "I didn't want the men to steal you."

"Right." The dark-haired cop shut his notebook and rose as did his partner. "We'll file the statement and start our investigation. Hopefully, there is a CCTV in the car park, which will help us with our inquiries."

Max stood too. "Thank you. I'll see you out and make sure the gate is closed."

Max escorted the cops to the gate, and immediately, the reporters burst into a hubbub of questions.

"Is it true you have a pet dragon?"

"Where do you keep a creature that large?"

"Is there a fire danger?"

Those were the questions he registered through the white noise. He gaped at the men and women, some of whom he knew through work and his contacts.

"Can we come inside and see the dragon?"

The cops exchanged a glance then focused on Max as they passed through the gateway to get to their vehicle.

Max shrugged. Hell, if he understood what they meant. The only thing their crazy questions did was confirm that he didn't want to work for the Edinburgh paper with its increasing tabloid stories. He wanted to do serious reporting on politics and break scandals to improve people's lives, not to increase the popularity of local celebrities. He glanced along the boundary that surrounded his property and noticed several reporters climbing the wall.

"Hey! This is private property. You can't enter without my permission."

The dark-haired cop was already behind the wheel of the police vehicle, but his red-haired buddy let out a shout. "You! Stop right there. The owner told you to leave. If you don't comply, I will issue you with a fine."

The trespassers climbed back to the public side of the fence with bad grace.

"We should be able to go after a story," one of the nearby reporters grumbled. "You can't stop us from writing about the dragon."

"Are you listening to yourself?" Max demanded. "You're all crazy. Dragons are fictional creatures. Storybook characters. Go home and give it a rest." With that, Max strode back to the house. He let himself inside and hesitated a beat before he locked the door.

"What's going on out there?" Sasha asked. "Why are there so many people?"

"They're convinced I'm harboring a dragon, keeping it hidden for my amusement. Idiots," Max snarled.

Noel appeared behind Sasha. "Shasha is a dragon."

"Yeah." Max dragged a tired hand through his hair. "I'll check the windows before I take a shower. My head is aching." He pressed his thumbs against his temples. "If you discover anyone peering through the windows, pull the curtains. And above all, don't talk to them. All right?"

"Yes, Max," Sasha said.

"Max sounds cranky," her dragon observed.

"He has a headache. We'll make him a tonic while he's taking a shower." She held out her hand to Noel. "Let's make some cookies.

I have some dough in the fridge."

While she made her headache potion, Noel busily cut out shapes with the cookie cutters Sasha had found in the cupboard. Luckily, she had everything she needed in the kitchen. Everything except one ingredient. Fresh chamomile. She hesitated before deciding. "You wait here, Noel, and don't move. I need to collect fresh herbs from the garden. If anyone knocks at the door, please ignore it."

He didn't look up, happy to play with the tiny bits of dough.

Sasha padded to the kitchen door and cocked her head. The babble of voices came from the reporters standing at the gate, but no other sounds reached her. At least, nothing to alarm her. She slid back the lock and opened the door. Seconds later, she slipped outside and headed for the vegetable patch. While she was out there, she plucked basil leaves, mint, and parsley along with the chamomile. She was halfway back to the house when two men confronted her. One snapped a photo, the bright light making her blink and her dragon complain. While she was recovering, the other man thrust a fluffy blue thing at her.

"What is that?" her dragon asked with mild curiosity. *"Touch the fluffy thing. It doesn't look edible."*

"What can you tell us about Max's pet dragon?" a man with a brown mustache and freckles asked.

"We're not a pet," her dragon said with disdain. *"Tell him."*

Mustache Man tried to push past her, but Sasha stood her ground. "Out. I believe Max told you this was personal property, and you have no right to enter."

"Push past," the man's companion said without a care for any laws. "She's a girl."

Anger built in Sasha, part of it fueled by her dragon. Impatient with the pesky men, Sasha gave one a forceful shove. He sailed through the air and hit with a thump.

Mustache Man didn't even bother looking to his friend's health and safety. Taller than her, he obviously fancied his chances of getting past her.

"Blow warning fire," her dragon snapped. *"This man is not getting to Max and Noel."*

Sasha gave her back garden a rapid scan and let her control cede toward her dragon. Her sight became sharper, and she knew Mustache Man would see her otherness in her eyes.

"Don't hurt him. Just frighten him," she warned.

"Yes. Yes," her dragon said, and her voice held glee.

When Mustache Man placed his hand on her shoulder, Sasha pushed him. He, too, went flying. Before he'd even landed, her dragon took more control and blew out a gust of fire. It landed right near Mustache Man's leg. His panicked yelp rippled through the air as she slammed the door.

"Take that," her dragon crowed.

They turned to discover Max gaping at them, blue eyes wide and shock emblazoned across his handsome face.

"What the fuck," he said.

CHAPTER 9

Oops! How Do We Fix This?

"*Now look what you've done,*" her dragon said. "*How are you going to fix this?*"

"*It was you, not me.*" Sasha swallowed hard. This was not the ideal way for Max to discover her other-self. What if he kicked her out of the house? Or worse, tossed her to the tabloid reporters who were baying like the bloodhounds they'd watched on telly last night.

"What was that?"

"Ah..."

Noel appeared behind him. He beamed at Sasha and ran to her, grabbing her around the legs and giving her a big hug. "Shasha scared away bad men. She saved me."

Max scrubbed a hand through his hair, closed his eyes briefly, then opened them. "I can't believe I'm saying this," he muttered. "You are a dragon."

"Yes," Sasha said in a small voice.

"A real live dragon."

"What does he expect? A paper one?" her dragon demanded in a snippy tone. *"One of those purple cartoon ones?"*

"Yes." Sasha waited for his next reaction.

"Crap," Max said. "This is something from the movies."

"Ah, I'll make a cup of tea," Sasha said.

"Why are we doing that?" her dragon asked.

"Because that's what they do on telly," Sasha muttered.

"What?" Max asked, sounding confused.

"Sorry. I forgot. I was talking to my dragon." She was aware Max watched her the entire time until she disappeared into the kitchen.

"Shasha, can I have chocolate?" Noel asked, running after her.

"Yes," she said, although, given the time, she should decide what to cook for dinner instead of making drinks.

Noel dragged out a chair at the kitchen table and climbed onto it to wait for his hot chocolate.

Max entered the kitchen, determination written on his handsome face.

"Such a pretty face," her dragon cooed. *"He doesn't look angry."*

No, but he wanted answers. She'd demand answers in the same circumstances.

Max dragged out a seat and picked up the envelope the cops had delivered. He tapped it on the tabletop.

Tap. Tap. Tap.

Each successive beat felt like a punishment. She didn't want to leave. She enjoyed spending her days with Noel and Max's kisses...well, she'd started to crave them.

"Where do you come from?" Max asked.

"An island called Perfume Isle. It's part of the Dragon Isles group."

"Where are they?"

"Off the coast of the mainland. Hundreds of years ago, dragon shifters lived among the humans here in the UK and Europe and farther afield. Humans made it a sport to kill us, and our numbers became drastically low. Our people retreated to the Dragon Isles, and they made a pact with the local druids who had a monastery on Smoking Isle. The druids produced a barrier, which stands between our worlds and keeps us invisible from the mainland. If any of your people venture too close, a sense of dread overcomes them, and they change course."

Sasha glanced at his impassive face and had no inkling of what he'd do next. She found his lack of expression unnerving and burst into further explanation.

"Somehow, I flew through the barrier. I landed on the beach

to orientate myself and discovered Noel. I couldn't leave a little boy alone in the dark, especially when he was crying. My dragon and I followed his tracks and brought him home. We didn't have anywhere to go, so we accepted your offer of shelter in return for looking after Noel."

"Is he mad at us?" her dragon asked. *"He's not saying anything."*

"Are you angry?" Sasha asked aloud. "If I'd told the truth, you would've thought I was crazy. I needed shelter, and you required help with Noel. I thought if I pretended to be a human, I'd eventually discover a way to get home."

Max rubbed his chin, his stubble rasping beneath his fingertips. "A dragon."

"I've done nothing to harm you or Noel." Sasha pressed a hand against her chest. "I'm sorry. What should I have done? Walked up to you and said, 'Hi, I'm a dragon.'?"

"But dragons aren't real."

A flash of anger filled her, and she let her dragon show in her eyes. "You kissed me. You weren't worried about dragons then."

Max pinched the bridge of his nose. His gaze met hers, and he flinched. "To be honest, I'm not certain what to think. You're right. You've protected Noel at every step and looked after him as if he were your own. I can't fault that. If you haven't hurt either of us so far, I figure you're not about to injure us in the future."

"We're not barbarians," her dragon snapped. *"Tell him. Tell him we're civilized and have honor."*

"Take care. You offend my dragon with your words. She says we are a civilized race and don't go around killing hapless humans."

"I apologize. That was thoughtless of me."

"It was," her dragon agreed. *"We won't let him kiss us again. Tell him."*

Sasha wanted more kisses. "Does this mean you won't kiss us again?"

Max groaned. "I'm so sorry. This has been a shock. Sasha, you're constantly on my mind, and the highlight of each day has been the contact with you and Noel. You faced down my grandmother. I know how forceful she can be, so I'm grateful for your strength of character and the way you stood up for Noel." His expression darkened. "Do you have any idea of the identity of those two men who tried to grab Noel?"

"I've never seen them before, although I have sensed someone observing us whenever we left the house."

"Why didn't you say something?" Max asked, his glower returning with force.

"When?" she demanded. "During your nightly calls, which are mainly for Noel? My dragon and I couldn't see anyone, which meant they kept their distance. Until today, Noel was safe. I'd intended to mention the situation to you when you came home again, which is what I've done."

Max opened his mouth again and obviously thought better of what he'd intended to say because his teeth clacked as he pressed his lips together. He huffed out a breath. "I don't know what to say. Under normal circumstances, I wouldn't want Noel anywhere near you. First, Grandmother would use this as a weapon to take Noel from me. Then there's the safety issue—"

"What safety issues?" Sasha snapped.

"Yeah." Her dragon lifted higher on Sasha's neck and onto her cheek so she could glare at Max and give him attitude. *"We love Noel. We'd never hurt him."*

Max gaped at her, and Sasha and her dragon glowered back.

"Is that your dragon?" he asked finally.

"Yes," she replied with a trace of impatience. "Look, everything we've done is to keep Noel safe and happy."

Max dragged his hand through his hair, and it wasn't for the first time since he'd arrived at home. His black hair stuck up, and Sasha hated to tell him his hair resembled the prickles of a hedgehog. "Please tell me about your dragon."

Sasha bristled, and her dragon followed suit.

Max backed up half a step. "Hell, I'm mishandling this. I'm sorry. Sasha's dragon, I'm sorry if my question is rude. Please help me understand."

"He's a human. He wouldn't comprehend our relationship," her dragon conceded. *"Explain to him."*

She agreed with her dragon. "My dragon is my other half, and we share a body. When we're in human form, my dragon resides on my outer body in her tattoo form. She normally rests on my chest, but she can move across my skin at will. When we're in dragon form, I'm in her—it's difficult to explain. In both forms, we communicate with each other telepathically."

"Two souls. One body. Got it, I think. Thank you for clarifying for me."

"Do you want us to leave?" Sasha asked in a small voice.

"Hot chocolate," Noel reminded Sasha.

Max stepped closer again. "No! You're right. It...this...you... This was a shock. You've given Noel first-rate care and made my last two helpers appear ordinary. And better, Noel's happy. Happier than I've seen him since Mum and Dad died, and that's down to you."

Sasha let out a shaky laugh, tension releasing from her muscles with a whoosh.

"*Woohoo!*" her dragon shouted. "*Let's make chocolate.*"

"Right. Hot chocolate. Sure thing. Noel, would you like to measure the ingredients for me? We'll all have chocolate," Sasha said.

"We'll add whisky to ours," Max said, standing. "I need a drink."

Sasha bustled around the kitchen, grabbing supplies and cups from the pantry. She helped Noel measure spoonfuls of chocolate mix, the familiar ritual soothing her inner angst.

"I'll add milk to Noel's," Max said. "Ours will work better with water."

Sasha nodded and followed Max's instructions.

"*What will we do now?*" her dragon asked. "*Maybe it's better for us to leave. We don't want to cause trouble for Max and Noel.*"

"*I don't know. If we must leave, at least we have some money, and we understand how things work here on the mainland.*"

A thump on the door indicated a visitor, and Max scowled. "I'll deal with our caller. We need to plan and work out how to get rid of the reporters."

Sasha handed Noel his hot chocolate while attempting to eavesdrop on the conversation.

"*It's those policemen again,*" her dragon said, and she slipped down Sasha's body until she rested in her usual spot over Sasha's heart, her tail curling over a hip.

An impassive Max directed two police officers into the kitchen, but Sasha saw one was a woman. "They want to talk to you about the abduction attempt."

"Okay," Sasha said with a polite smile. Best not to offer information but to wait for the questions and give them enough that they didn't get suspicious. On the other hand, not too much info either.

"Have a seat," Max said. "Would you like a hot drink? Tea or coffee?"

"No, thanks," the policewoman said. Her blonde hair coiled neatly at the back of her neck, and her expression was so severe that worry rolled through Sasha. "We have your statement. I want to go through it again in case you remember something you missed earlier."

"Sure," Sasha said.

The policewoman asked her questions, and she described again what had happened and everything she'd seen.

"There were also reports of a dragon. Can you tell me anything about that?"

Sasha laughed and made her eyes grow wide. "A dragon?" she spluttered.

The policewoman tapped her pen against her notebook. "Yes." Her tone was dry. "That is what locals are reporting."

Sasha wrinkled her nose, shot a quick glance at Noel, and hoped he didn't tell them she was a dragon.

Max must've thought the same thing since he stood. "Do you need me for anything? Noel works better with a routine, and it's time for his shower."

"Go ahead. We're almost finished," the policewoman said.

Max whisked Noel away, and Sasha and her dragon relaxed a fraction.

"The reporters outside are saying the dragon landed here," the policewoman said.

"What?" Sasha's jolt was entirely natural and not manufactured. "Where?" She gazed toward the window and peered outside at the back garden. "Are they saying the dragon is inside the house? What are they drinking? That's crazy."

The policeman, who had remained silent until now, snorted.

The policewoman sent him a silencing glare before turning back to Sasha. "Would you mind if we searched the house and grounds?"

"That should be okay," Sasha said. "But you should check with Max first since he owns the house."

"What exactly is your position here?"

"I'm Max's fiancée," Sasha said, "and I also look after Noel when Max needs to work in Edinburgh."

The policewoman glanced at the ring on Sasha's left hand. "Congratulations. How long have you been engaged?"

"A few months," Sasha said.

"Do you have a date for the wedding?"

"*Careful,*" her dragon warned.

"*I've got this,*" Sasha said with a bright smile. "Max's parents died in an accident several months ago. It didn't seem respectful to set a date and marry straightaway. I wanted Noel more settled, and both Max and I wanted to enjoy our wedding. I mean, you only have one day, and it should be special."

Max returned to grab his phone.

"Max, the police want to search the house and grounds," Sasha said.

"Why?" Max barked. "We have done nothing wrong."

"No, sir," the policewoman said. "But the reporters outside insist that a dragon landed here."

"They think we're hiding a dragon inside the house?" Max scoffed. "I've never heard anything so ridiculous in my life. Aren't dragons meant to be massive creatures? How would one fit inside the house without knocking down a wall?"

The policeman barked out a laugh, which the policewoman quelled with a glare.

"You're welcome to search the grounds if you must, but even you must admit the idea of a live dragon entering my house and cowering under the bed is crazy."

"Are you refusing to let us search the house?" the policewoman persisted.

"You have no legal reason to search my home," Max said calmly. "To say you're searching for a dragon is plain ridiculous. If you wish to search, you'll need a warrant."

"Because you're hiding something," the policewoman shot back.

Max stood his ground, not intimidated in the slightest. "Like what?"

"Someone suggested, Mr. Lombardy, that you staged the abduction attempt on your brother."

Sasha's mouth dropped open in shock while Max appeared equally astonished by the allegation.

"Who suggested that?" Max demanded.

"Your grandmother," the policewoman said, watching him closely.

"Out," Max said, jerking his head toward the door. "Leave my property. I've changed my mind about you searching any part of my home or garden."

"But it's not your property, is it, sir?" the policewoman said in a smooth tone. "The house is in trust for your younger brother, and you only live here because you're his legal guardian."

"Out." Max enforced the order by walking to the doorway, which led to the passage and the front door. "I don't have to listen to these accusations. If you want to search this house, you bring a search warrant."

CHAPTER 10

Grandmother Makes Her Move

Max escorted the two cops out while Sasha jogged upstairs to check on Noel. As she approached the bathroom, the garbled words of a song drifted to her—one Noel had learned at kindergarten. She grinned because his singing was horrid, but he was enjoying himself.

"Hey, Noel. Did you wash behind your ears?"

Her dragon chortled. *"That's what our mother always asked us."*

"Yeah," Sasha replied ruefully.

"Shasha, I'm hungry."

"Me, too," Sasha agreed. "We'll cook dinner once you dress in warm clothes."

Sasha helped Noel to dry himself and dress, then they walked down to the kitchen. Max was sitting at the table, reading the contents of the envelope the police officers had delivered. A deep scowl dug into his forehead.

"Is something wrong?"

Max shot a glance at Noel. "We'll talk once Noel is in bed."

"Watch TV?" Noel asked.

Sasha exchanged a glance with Max.

"Let him watch a cartoon," he said. "If I don't talk about this, I'm going to burst. Come on, buddy. Which cartoon would you like to see tonight?"

"What are we cooking for dinner?" her dragon asked. *"It might be better if we leave the chicken for another night."*

"Remember, we watched how to cut a chicken up into portions. If we do that, it will cook faster," Sasha said. *"We'll have it with mashed potatoes, peas, and gravy."* She set to work and soon had the chicken in the oven. With that done, she peeled the potatoes and cut them small.

Max entered the kitchen, and the cackle of Noel's favorite cartoon dog drifted after him.

"Thank you for starting dinner," Max said. He tipped his half-drunk hot chocolate in the sink. "The letter the cops brought and had me sign for are legal papers. My grandmother is upping the ante. She says I'm hardly here with Noel and that I leave his

168

care to my au pair."

"What's an au pair?"

"A person who looks after children and receives a payment for it," Max said. "She doesn't believe we're engaged."

"She's right," Sasha said, even though the words made her chest ache.

Max groaned. "God, I'm so confused. I have feelings for you, and every time I look at you, all I want to do is steal a kiss."

"What's stopping him?" her dragon whispered. *"We're gorgeous."*

Sasha wanted the answer to the question too. "Why don't you kiss me?"

Max met her gaze, his eyes full of honesty. "Until I saw you spurt fire at that reporter, I'd intended to kiss you."

"What changed?"

"You're a weredragon," he said.

"We call ourselves dragon shifters," Sasha corrected. "From the reading we've done since our arrival, a weredragon is the same being, no matter which form they take. We are two beings in a single body. One of us cannot thrive without the other."

"I'll remember that."

"You should. Some dragons can be particularly snooty and full of pride. Questioning their origins is considered rude."

Max lost some of his color. "Would your family approve of me?"

Sasha died a little inside.

"We can't lose Max," her dragon said. *"We like kissing him! We*

169

must have more Max kisses."

"My brothers will like you." The truth.

"But not your parents? Don't you want to go home? My world is here. Noel is here."

"The day we came through the barrier, my mother had informed me that because I'd turned down all offers of marriage to date, my parents had arranged a betrothal for me."

"You're betrothed?"

Sasha shrugged. "I guess I am. Officially." She checked on the chicken, the meaty aroma overlaid with herbs making her stomach rumble. "Bruceous is the same age as my parents. He is wealthy, and his previous wife died in an accident several years ago. He's not a nice dragon. He's the type who goes around trapping younger women in corners or slyly pinching their bottoms."

"That's sexual harassment."

"Yes," Sasha agreed as she placed the pot of potatoes on the stove to boil. "But somehow he persuaded my parents he'd make an excellent match for me. My gut says that the moment we're together, he'll be ready to chase the next shiny object."

"That's what your parents want for you?"

"They mean well," Sasha said. "To them, he's a gentleman with an important position in the community. My dragon and I haven't tried very hard to return, mainly because we've been responsible for Noel's safety. But if we'd wanted to badly enough, we could've crept out at night to investigate the barrier. Once again, we worried that would leave Noel alone if we penetrated the barrier."

Max cursed and bounded to his feet. "I'm a selfish oaf only thinking of myself and what this news means to me." When he reached her, he hugged her hard. "Every step of the way, you've given Noel and me your loyalty. He is thriving under your care."

"What are you going to do about your grandmother?" Sasha asked.

"I don't know," Max said in a harsh voice. "According to the legal papers, the judge has ordered me to hand over Noel on the first of the month."

"That's in two days."

"Yes, and it sounds as if this decision is final, that the judge has made a ruling based on the information Julia provided. The legal papers state I must leave the premises."

"That's not fair. Why is your grandmother doing this?" Sasha asked. "You're family. You should pull together, not fight each other."

"I agree."

"Perhaps you should investigate the reasons behind your grandmother's determination to get custody of Noel."

"I thought... I mean, she told me she thought my lifestyle as a bachelor didn't work with a young child. She worried I'd palm him off on a stranger."

"Which is what you did," Sasha said without heat. "She suspects the validity of our engagement because it happened suddenly. She wonders why she didn't know of my existence earlier."

Max snorted. "It's not as if we've ever been close. My grandparents disapproved of my father. The fact my mother was pregnant with me when my parents married upset them greatly. Julia, my grandmother, wanted Mum to marry a family friend with a title."

"Can I read the document?" Sasha asked.

Max shoved them across the table toward her. "Have at it. I'll check on dinner."

Sasha read the legal document carefully.

"Does she have money problems?" her dragon asked.

"Excellent question," Sasha said aloud. "My dragon wonders if your grandparents are in debt. Noel comes with money and property to enable his upkeep, but whoever becomes his guardian ends up with the use of that wealth."

Max turned from his position at the stove, a fork in his hand. "My father's family have money and live in Surrey. I always thought my mother's parents were reasonably well off. Comfortable, at least."

"Perhaps they were, but could that have changed without your knowledge? Can you ask someone you trust to check for you?"

"Maybe you're right," Max drawled. "I have a friend in Edinburgh. Jerome is a private investigator. I'll ask him to start digging."

"Will there be enough time? The papers give your grandparents the right to take Noel in two days." She scowled. "Why wouldn't they consider what Noel wants?"

"He's a child. He's only four, and he has Down syndrome," Max said with a trace of bitterness.

"Can you fight this?"

"I don't know. If I let them take Noel, I'll have a hell of a fight on my hands to get him back. If there's any chance my grandmother is using Noel to get money instead of acting in this way for the greater benefit..." He trailed off with a shake of his head, his knuckles white around the fork he held.

"There are a few other options," Sasha said slowly, her mind busy working on solutions. "We could get married and present a united front. We might be young, but I believe Noel is happy with us."

"What about your betrothed?"

Sasha snorted. "A horrid fate. If I end up with Bruceous, I'll turn into a bitter old maid."

Max sent her a thoughtful look. "And would this marriage be a real one?"

"If you're amiable to marriage with a dragon shifter," Sasha said, seeking her words with care. "My dragon and I both like you. We're attracted to you."

"And we want to experiment with him—try the things from the kissing books," her dragon said with enthusiasm.

Sasha flinched, and she watched Max's gaze narrow. Interest

glittered in him, and his features took on a predatory air.

"Like me?"

"We miss you when you're not here," Sasha said.

Max laughed. "Noel misses me."

"We imagine kissing you and more," Sasha admitted, deciding to go with the truth rather than acting the blushing maiden.

"If we got married," Max said, "I'd expect a real marriage. Would you still want to go home?"

"I don't know. I miss my family, and my absence will worry them. The chicken smells as if it's almost cooked. Let me check it."

"You can smell that?"

Sasha laughed. "Yes." Her humor faded. "Max, what are we going to do?"

"No idea." Max brushed a quick kiss on her lips and moved out of her way. "I'll check on Noel and ring my private investigator friend. That's a start, but two days isn't much time."

"It's not fair that she has used our friendship to force you from your home."

Max snorted. "Given that the judge has instructed me to vacate the house, my guess is my grandparents will move in here with Noel."

Sasha focused on creating their meal and chopped green herbs to add to the mashed potatoes.

"I enjoy preparing food," her dragon said.

"Me too," Sasha said. *"Do you remember the tales Mother told us*

of the islands? I mean, before the barrier came into existence?"

"There were four islands, but those in charge decided we'd occupy three of them because the humans on the fourth island didn't wish to lose their contact with the mainland."

Max returned to the kitchen. "I've contacted my friend. Jerome will do some online research tonight and dig around a bit more tomorrow."

Sasha shot Max a quick glance. "Would you consider taking Noel and running?"

"I'd get caught," Max said without hesitation. "They'd have my car registration and find us easily. Even though I'd love to thumb my nose at my grandmother, running isn't the answer."

"What if I shifted to a dragon and flew you and Noel to Holy Island?" Sasha said, speaking slowly as she and her dragon mentally finessed their plan. "While the cops might object, it would give your private investigator friend time to check out your grandparents and perhaps discover the reasons behind their actions. No one has photos of a dragon—not that I've seen—therefore they have no proof of their existence."

Max was silent for a while. "If the barrier sucks you in and throws you back to your world, what happens then?"

"You and Noel would be safe from your grandparents."

"I wouldn't have any money or a way of earning a living," Max said.

"My family would help you. My brothers. You'd be safe."

"What about your betrothal?"

"I thought we'd keep pretending." Unaccustomed heat speared through her. "We'd have to share a room, and you'd need to take on our scent before my family would believe me. The pretense would be harder in my world because dragons have exceptional hearing and an excellent sense of smell."

"And if we're discovered, or your parents attack me and ask questions later? Or the dragon who wants you takes issue with me?"

"They'd have to go through us," her dragon snapped.

Sasha laughed aloud. "My dragon and I are of one accord. They'd have to injure us to get to you or Noel. You are ours to protect." She turned away to take the chicken from the oven. Next, she picked up the pot to drain the potatoes.

"Let me think about it," Max said finally. "You might not manage to return to your world."

"That's true, but I haven't tried."

"God, I was so lucky when you walked into my life," he said. "Most of the kids around here of your age wouldn't have given a second thought if they'd found Noel alone. They wouldn't have noticed his distress."

"I'm not a kid. But the humans here might've surprised you and acted on Noel's behalf."

Max snorted. "They might have contacted the police, which would've meant trouble for me."

Max's phone buzzed. "It's Jerome," he said to Sasha before answering the call. "That was quick. Have you discovered something for me already?"

Sasha added butter and milk to the potatoes and mashed them while listening to the conversation. Max's friend had a low, gravelly voice.

"Your grandmother has gambling debts," he said.

"How big?"

"Big enough that she can't pay them. They've mortgaged their house to the hilt, and they've failed to make the last two payments. I suspect the bank was putting pressure on them, so she resorted to a loan shark. They want their money back."

"How did you learn this so fast?" Max asked. "I didn't have a clue."

"Contacts."

"He's secretive," her dragon said.

"It's his job to trade in information," Sasha countered. *"It makes sense for him to keep secrets."*

"Also, the judge who signed the documents is a family friend of your grandparents."

"Crap," Max said. "They're saying Sasha and I are not in a relationship, and my grandparents insist I'm using her as a childminder instead of spending quality time with Noel."

"In my opinion, your grandparents want to exploit Noel to get their hands on the extra money that should go to your brother's upkeep," the friend said.

"Can you give me the info so I can prove this?" Max asked.

"I thought you'd want the truth. Information. I doubt my contact will stand up to bat for you. Sorry."

"I understand," Max said. "Send me your bill, and I'll pay it straight away."

"Next time," Jerome said. "This one is gratis. I hate that your family is doing this to you and Noel. I know you love the little tyke."

"Thanks," Max said, his voice catching. "Appreciate it."

"Catch ya later," Jerome said and hung up without another word.

"I heard," Sasha said before Max could speak. "What are you going to do?"

"Not sure, although I'm not inclined to let my grandmother win. She doesn't care about Noel. If Jerome is correct, all she wants is the money."

"Dinner is ready," Sasha said. "Call Noel for me while I dish up."

Max wandered off, and she heard him and Noel discussing the washing of hands.

"Max and Noel should come with us," her dragon said.

"He has to consider Noel's safety, his well-being. We don't even know if we can get back through the barrier. If that's the case, leaving and remaining trapped here would be a problem."

"I don't want to leave Max," her dragon said.

Sasha sighed as she served the chicken and added potatoes and peas to each plate. "We forgot the gravy. Let me heat it in the microwave."

In no time at all, the three of them were sitting down to dinner.

"Yum," Noel said. "Thank you, Shasha."

She grinned. "You're welcome."

They didn't discuss dragons or grandparents during dinner or afterward. Max put Noel to bed, read him a dragon story, and came downstairs to help her with the dishes.

"I peeked outside," she said. "I saw one car, and it looked as if the men inside were asleep."

When they finished the dishes, Max said, "Let's turn off this light and turn on the one in the family room. We'll pretend we're relaxing for the evening but creep outside. I want to check the garden for lurking reporters."

"Why?" Sasha asked.

"Because the more I think about this situation, the angrier I become. I'm considering asking my friend to uncover proof of my grandmother's debts so I can refute their charges. I have two days before I have to hand over Noel and move from this house. There is nothing to stop us from visiting Holy Island and returning."

"Won't the reporters follow you?"

"Not if we take the mode of transport you suggested," Max said. "I'll need more cash and an idea of a place to book for accommodation. I can get one of my friends to book it for us.

Jerome would do it."

"And if I can find a way through the barrier?" Sasha asked. "I'm not sure I'm ready to go home. I like it here with you." She caught Max's gaze and held it. "You and Noel feel like home."

"You are so sweet," Max said, standing and going to her. He grasped her hand and tugged her to the couch, where he sat her on his knee. "I don't know what I did to deserve you, but the thought of you leaving makes me want to howl."

"We go together," Sasha whispered.

"It's not as if I have anything to tie me here. Only Noel." Max wrapped his arms around her, and peace seemed to settle over him. "An adventure it is."

CHAPTER 11

The Cool Flight

Max rang his PI friend to arrange accommodation and the ongoing investigation. Between him and Sasha, they discovered they had enough cash to cover any expenses for the weekend. Jerome answered the phone, and Max told him some of what he intended to do.

"Are you making a run for it?" his friend asked.

Max didn't hesitate to give Jerome honesty. "Not sure at this stage. I'm thinking about it, but I don't know for certain what I'm going to do. I love Noel, and I doubt my grandmother wants him because she loves him. She sees an opportunity."

"What about the house and contents?" his friend asked.

"If Sasha and I decide not to return, I'll send a key to your post office box."

"Make sure you disable your phone GPS and try not to use it unless it's an emergency." He rattled off an email address. "Remember that address, and if you need to contact me, do it via email. Other than that, don't use your credit card. Use cash. Try to change your appearance and ditch your car if you can. Borrow a friend's car. You can take mine if you want."

"No, I don't need a vehicle where we're going. If we decide to come back, no one would be any the wiser." Unless they spotted a dragon wheeling through the sky.

"Contact me if you need me," Jerome said. "I don't like what your grandmother is doing to you. I'm here to help as much as I can."

"Thanks. What is the best way to pay you?"

"Send a retainer direct to my bank account. If anyone questions me, I'll tell them the truth. That you contacted me to investigate your grandmother because you were suspicious about her motives with Noel."

Max hesitated then gave his friend as much truth as he could. "I'm not sure if I'll be able to contact you. I mean, if I run, but I give you my oath I'll somehow pay everything I owe you."

"Don't worry about it," Jerome said, his voice gruff with emotion. "I know you won't leave me hanging. We're friends, and if I know anything about you, it's that you're loyal and have integrity." He barked out a laugh. "I've no idea how you lasted at the tabloid press in Edinburgh."

"I walked out when I discovered my grandmother had a hand in me getting that job," Max confessed. "She used my boss to make sure I spent time away from Noel, so she could tell the judge I left him with strangers."

"There's a rumor going around you're engaged."

"Where did you—? Never mind. Yeah. Sasha is amazing."

"But you didn't become engaged months ago," his friend commented.

"Maybe not, but that doesn't mean what I feel for Sasha isn't genuine."

"You're going to marry her?"

"We're taking things slow, but Noel and I adore her. She's amazing." Max laughed. "Glad I met her before you did."

"All right. Send me a message if you can, and I'll keep digging until I have enough to detonate your grandmother's plan. The trouble will be finding someone willing to talk."

"I understand. Do your best," Max said. "Thanks."

Max hung up, and a noise had him jerking up his head. "Sasha." God, she was beautiful with her blue eyes and copper-brown hair. Seconds later, his hands rested on her shoulders, and she grinned up at him.

"What?"

"Noel and I are lucky to have you in our lives."

Her smile faded. "What about my dragon?"

"Admittedly, that part is more difficult to get my head around, but Noel understood what you were all this time. He kept telling me you were a dragon. I didn't grasp he meant it literally, but he's not frightened of you in the slightest. I'd say he has a case of hero-worship."

"Wait until he meets my big brothers," Sasha said. "I've packed a bag for Noel and pulled out warm clothes for him to wear. Flying will be cold, so you and Noel need to dress in as many layers as you can manage. Pack what you can in a light bag you can wear on your back. You'll need to hold Noel and sit behind him. I can carry luggage in my talons."

Max frowned. "Have you done this before? How do you know you can carry me?"

Sasha paused and cocked her head as if she was listening. A slow, sexy grin curved her lips, and everything inside Max turned molten hot. When he stared into her eyes, he glimpsed a hint of otherness, yet it didn't scare him. Instead, intrigue joined the lust simmering inside him. This mysterious woman entertained him, consoled him, challenged him, and he understood at that moment what he'd missed in previous relationships.

Intelligence and empathy, along with the elusive *something* that told him he'd never get bored at Sasha's side. Now, if only her family approved of him and accepted Noel. If that didn't happen, he couldn't see a way forward for them. He wanted to ask Sasha to marry him, and he wished to do the old-fashioned thing and ask for her father's approval.

Her smile had grown wider while his thoughts had roamed to his future plans.

"Why are you grinning at me like that?"

"My dragon insulted you."

Max's brows rose. "She did? Why?"

"You expressed concern about us being able to carry you. You implied we're weak. My dragon states we are not only gorgeous, but we are strong and could squash a puny human without breaking a sweat. We would, however, look after Noel if something happened to you because we like Noel very much."

"Well, I'm glad to hear that," Max said dryly. "I'll pack. Do we need to take any food?"

"I'll pack a few things—some of Noel's favorites. The locals on Holy Island come over here to shop for groceries."

"All right. I'll pack food in my bag and put on as many clothes as I can manage. From memory, there is a pub and a few small shops. We can't use my credit card because that will allow the police to track us, so we must rely on cash."

Max's phone rang, and when he saw it was Jerome, he answered. "Have you found a place for us to stay?"

"I have. It's on the outskirts of town. The owner said she has to attend a funeral tomorrow, but she'll leave the key in her mailbox for you to collect. Told me the causeway was open early tomorrow morning, and she was heading to the mainland. I paid for two days."

"Thank you," Max said, his thanks heartfelt.

"The tide is right for you to cross early in the morning. Anything else I can do for you?"

"No, just get enough dirt on my grandmother to stop her from taking Noel. I appreciate this more than I can say."

"Introduce me to your girl."

"After we're married," Max said.

Jerome chortled and was still laughing when Max disconnected the call. Aware of the ticking clock, Max grabbed his day pack from the hall cupboard and headed to his bedroom. He stuffed his tablet inside plus spare underwear and socks. He donned his hiking clothes since he always dressed in layers when walking.

In the kitchen, he packed the cans and packets of food Sasha had placed on the table.

"That should do it," Sasha said. "You wake Noel, and I'll go outside to check for anyone skulking around the yard. We'll leave from the back garden since it will give us more cover until I take to the air."

Max nodded and took off to grab Noel. To himself, he confessed to nerves since dragons were an unknown quality. While he knew and trusted Sasha, he wasn't so sure about her dragon.

"Hey, Noel," Max shook his brother gently. "Wake up, buddy. Sasha is taking us for a dragon ride."

Typically difficult to wake, the mention of Sasha and her dragon seemed to do the trick.

"We have to dress you warmly because Sasha says flying can be cold for us. I think her scales keep her warm, but we need to wear extra clothes otherwise, our teeth will chatter.

Max realized he was prattling like a champion, a sure sign of nerves, and he clicked his teeth together and shut his mouth.

"Where is Shasha?"

"Getting ready. She has packed food for us since we're going to fly to an island and stay there for two days. We're going on an adventure."

With Noel dressed in as many clothes as he could tug onto his brother's wriggly body, Max led him downstairs. He bent to fit a pair of runners on Noel's feet and picked up his day pack. It was bloody heavy, but Max didn't complain. They needed this preparation, and it would be best if they kept to themselves as much as possible on the island. He led Noel outside.

Sasha walked stealthily through the shadows and appeared at Max's side before he realized it was her.

"Two cars containing sleeping reporters. If we hurry, we can disappear before anyone misses us," she said.

Max's stomach did an uncharacteristic swoop. He was nervous, which he hated to admit, but it was expected, right? He'd never seen a dragon—not in person. Heck, before today, he'd considered them a part of myth and legend. His stomach bucked again, and he forced himself to speak. "What do we need to do?"

"Stand back, so I can morph to a dragon. I'd hate to hurt either you or Noel by mistake."

Max grasped Noel's hand, and they stepped back against the side of the house.

"Is Shasha turning into a dragon?" Noel asked in a loud voice.

"Shush," Max said and crouched beside his brother. "We have to be quiet, so we don't wake the reporters sleeping in their cars. If they get a photo of Sasha, she'll be in trouble. Okay?"

Noel gave a solemn nod, his gaze on Sasha. Max rose and turned to face Sasha too. Whoa! The woman was naked! For a stunned moment, Max gaped at her shapely body. She was crouching and stuffing her clothes into a cloth bag. When she stood, his eyes widened further. A bronze dragon tattoo covered most of her torso, and as he stared, the tattoo shifted on Sasha's body and winked at him.

He must've made a noise because Sasha grinned and looked straight at him.

"My dragon says she told you we were gorgeous. Are you ready? Once I shift, I want you to climb onto my back and sit near my shoulders, just in front of my wings. Seat Noel before you so you can hold on to him."

Max nodded, mesmerized by the golden—no, it was more bronze—dragon that was now waving at him and blowing kisses. He shook himself. "Where do you want me to put the bags you need to carry?"

"Leave Noel's bag near my cloth one."

Max darted across the lawn to place Noel's pack with Sasha's.

"Max, everything will be all right," Sasha said.

Unable to help himself, he strode across the gap separating them, placed his hands on her shoulders, and gave her a quick but firm kiss. "You *are* gorgeous," he murmured. "Both of you."

Then he was striding back to Noel and taking his brother's hand. "Are you ready?" he asked Noel.

His brother grunted, his blue eyes gleaming in the scant light. His round face held eagerness and excitement and none of the apprehension that clawed at Max's belly. So many things could go wrong. He was placing a tremendous amount of trust in Sasha... Hell, from the start, he'd trusted her with Noel, and he needed to continue instead of letting fear get the better of him. But even so, there were so many variables at play. The reporters might see them and get photos of Sasha. Heck, pictures of him and Noel with Sasha would give his grandmother more ammunition. Then there was the fact he was leaving the house. His grandmother and her team of lawyers might take umbrage with his absence. And, finally, he didn't know what to do for the best.

For Noel or himself.

Yep, the variables were doing his head.

Max hadn't considered how Sasha would shift to her dragon form or what it would look like. He'd read books, seen movies that depicted the process for werewolves. This was not as he imagined. Sasha's shift was fast and seamless. One moment a strikingly beautiful and naked woman stood before them, and the next, a bronze dragon. It had an immense body covered with bronze scales. A long neck and largish head. Sasha's eyes were also blue with black slits instead of pupils. Intelligence gleamed from her, and she slowly flitted long eyelashes at him.

She crouched in front of him, her nostrils flaring. A tiny puff of smoke emerged.

Noel darted forward and stroked her hide, unafraid of the gigantic dragon. Shrugging inwardly, Max fitted his pack to his back and lifted Noel onto Sasha's shoulders. He sat astride between two dangerous, gleaming spikes. Max clambered up behind Noel in an ungainly fashion.

In the next moment, they were off. Somehow, Sasha scooped up the two other bags in her talons. Her wings flapped, lifting them into the air. Noel released a chortle of pleasure. Max was more worried about the reporters seeing them, but all remained quiet as they flew away from the house.

In mere seconds, they were flying over the sea. The wind whipped their hair, and Max wished he'd thought to don gloves. Sasha had been right to warn them about the cold.

Holy Island soon lay beneath them. Scattered lights glowed from houses and buildings. They'd checked a paper map of the area instead of going online and had figured out the best landing place was the middle of the island. It would mean they'd need to walk to get to their accommodation, but given the hour, Max doubted many residents would be driving around to notice them.

By the time Sasha swooped downward, Max's face had gone numb. They'd decided not to fly near the settlement either for fear of someone spotting them flying over. Not that the town was substantial. Max had visited as a child with his parents and on a school trip.

Sasha landed in a field, and Max slid down before reaching up to lift Noel free.

Noel clapped his hands, his expression full of pleasure despite the late hour. "Again," he insisted.

"Sasha needs to have a rest first," Max said, making his voice firm. His little brother wasn't beyond begging or having a hissy fit to get his way when he became overtired.

Thankfully, Noel allowed Max to pluck him from Sasha's back.

Sasha transformed as quickly as the last time. This time she shivered and hurriedly rifled through her bag to grab her clothes. She pulled on black trousers, a shirt, and a jacket without bothering about underwear. She took the time to pull on socks, though before she donned her boots. "We're near the accommodation your friend booked for us. I landed closer than we'd planned, so it should be a five-minute walk at most."

"Let's hope the owner was as efficient as she promised, and the key is in her mailbox." Max pulled a face. "Otherwise, we'll be in trouble."

Sasha picked up her bag plus Noel's.

"Let me take that," Max said.

"I think you're going to need to carry Noel. Now the excitement is over, he's drooping."

Seeing she was right, Max lifted Noel and sat him on his shoulders.

Sasha led the way, her progress unfaltering despite the dark. Max hadn't thought to bring a torch.

"You're very quiet," Sasha said after a while.

"I'm unsure of what to do for the best. For Noel."

"You can't let your grandmother get her hands on him, not if all she's interested in is the trust money," Sasha said.

"But we can't spend our life running either," Max said.

"You can't let her win."

"No. My mind is chasing in circles."

"Let's try to enjoy the two days we have before the court's deadline. Perhaps a third alternative will come to us," Sasha said. "Ah, I think that's the cottage we've rented, judging by the photos your friend sent to my email address. Why don't you and Noel wait here, and I'll run to get the key?"

Max smothered a yawn and indicated acceptance of the plan. She headed into the darkness without hesitation and was back in under ten minutes, flourishing a key. "Found it along with a note."

"Great. I want to get Noel in bed, otherwise it will be a fun day for all of us tomorrow."

With a nod, Sasha unlocked the door and flicked on the entrance light to reveal a large room sectioned into seating, dining, and food preparation areas.

"*Nice,*" her dragon said. "*I like the human's open rooms instead of lots of smaller ones. I enjoy the space.*"

"*Me too,*" Sasha agreed.

Max dumped his pack on the floor, picked up Noel's smaller bag and led his brother down a passage leading off the principal room. She picked up Max's pack and took out their food supplies.

"*What was in the note?*" her dragon asked.

Sasha plucked it out of her pocket and read the contents. "Excellent," she murmured. "Fresh milk, eggs, bacon, and bread. That means we won't need to go out if we don't want to—not to visit the town at any rate."

Max came out a few minutes later.

"Is Noel asleep?"

"For a while there, I thought he'd put up a fight. The flight thrilled him, and he wanted to draw a picture of your dragon before he forgot the details." Max pulled a face. "He fell asleep midway through telling me about exploring the island. These days, he's excited and involved, and it's all thanks to you. I hate to think of him going backward with my grandparents. I'm sure they'd look after him, and he'd lack for nothing physically, but their child-rearing methods are old-fashioned. Seen and not heard. Noel needs to learn and repeat things until he understands them. I want him to be excited by life."

Sasha touched his forearm and squeezed. "Noel is a great kid. He has lots of friends. He's well-behaved, although sometimes stubborn. My dragon is stubborn, too."

"Huh!" her dragon said but confined her comments to that.

"You didn't see him after Mum and Dad died. You've worked miracles with Noel."

"Jerome arranged for the owner to stock up on breakfast food. We have milk, tea, and coffee, along with bacon and eggs. A few other treats too."

"Something else," Max said. "There is one other bedroom with an enormous bed, admittedly, but if we both want comfort, we'll have to share."

"Tell him he's safe," her dragon murmured. *"We're too tired to attack his body."*

Sasha chuckled.

Max's brows rose. "What?"

"My dragon confirmed you're safe. We're as exhausted as Noel."

"Then, we'll share."

"Yes," Sasha said without hesitation, although her stomach did a slow flip of anticipation.

"Let's go then," Max said. "You can use the bathroom first."

"I wouldn't mind a shower," Sasha said. "We're sweaty after the flight over to the island."

"Did you sense your barrier?"

"Yes, it was there. Intact. Honestly, I have no idea how we crossed through." She stopped in the middle of the passage. "What if I can never return?"

"We'll try to find a way for you, Sasha, but you will always have a home with Noel and me."

"While I didn't part on great terms with my mother, I miss my family."

"I get it. I miss my parents too." Max folded her into a hug, and Sasha melted against him, accepting the comfort he offered.

"We'll go for a walk tomorrow. Perhaps we'll find something to help you get home. A clue."

"*Suddenly, I am not tired,*" her dragon said, her tone distinctly flirtatious. "*This man is decent. I bet he wouldn't go around pinching other dragon's backsides.*"

Max pulled away from her, smiled, and kissed her lips. He shunted her toward the bathroom. "I'll bring your bag to you. You'll want your clothes."

"We normally sleep in our skin."

Max stilled and waited for a beat before speaking. "Please, for my sake, wear something to bed this once."

"Fine," Sasha said.

"I'll leave your bag outside the door."

"*Aw, he's so sweet,*" her dragon cooed. "*A gentleman.*"

"Thanks," Sasha said.

The water was hot, and she enjoyed her shower immensely. After donning a long T-shirt, she padded down the passage to the bedroom. She found Max stretched out on the bed, fast asleep. He wasn't snoring, but his loud breaths were close.

Shrugging, Sasha let him be.

"At least we can take off our T-shirt and get under the blankets," her dragon said. *"You know I prefer to sleep without clothes because—"*

"Because you suffer clothes during the day when you're certain most dragons and humans would prefer to study your sexy dragon form," Sasha finished. She'd listened to the argument so many times she could repeat it verbatim.

In the interest of peace—because she was truly exhausted—she shed her T-shirt and slid under the covers.

She pushed away her fears of becoming trapped on this side of the barrier forever and fell asleep almost immediately.

It was still dark when she awoke. She found herself pressed up against a male chest.

"Mmm, nice," her dragon said drowsily. *"I like Max trespassing on our side of the bed."*

Sasha focused. *"Ah, newsflash. We seem to have gravitated toward Max, not the other way around."*

"Well, you could never call us stupid," her dragon said with satisfaction. *"It's a pity our parents didn't give us the benefit of*

the doubt and let us choose our partner. We found Max, and he's exceptional."

"He's not a dragon."

"Doesn't matter. We could still have children with Max if we wanted and live in either world. We've proved we're adaptable and clever enough to blend in here."

"Max mightn't want children."

"Pffff! He loves Noel and has given up a lot to raise him. Max didn't have to fight for his brother. He could've let his grandparents take care of Noel. Even though he had an important job in that London place, he gave it up. He changed his life and walked away from his fiancée."

"True." Sasha yawned, hoping her dragon had ended her lecture.

"You have to act positive and reach for what you want in this life."

Sasha bit back a groan. Evidently not.

"So far, we've escaped Bruceous, whom we do not want as a husband. Max is an acceptable husband," her dragon persisted.

"What if we can go home? What then? If Max came with us, what if our parents force him to leave and refuse to let us stay together because he's a human?"

Her dragon didn't reply for a beat, and some of the building tension slipped from Sasha. Her dragon didn't have an argument for that. It wasn't as if crossing between their worlds was possible. Her presence on this side of the barrier was unusual. She'd never heard of another dragon leaving the Dragon Isles.

"We could seduce him and get pregnant with his young," her dragon said. *"He'd never leave us then. He's too honorable."*

"No!" Sasha blurted, shocked to her core by the suggestion. "I'd never try to trap a mate in that way. It's wrong and no better than our parents trying to foist Bruceous on us."

"Who are you talking to?" Max grumbled. His warm breath feathering against her collarbone, making her shiver.

"Um, sorry. I didn't realize I spoke aloud. My dragon and I are having a difference of opinion about the way to discover a mate."

"What did your dragon suggest?" Max asked, sounding more alert now.

"You don't want to know."

"Actually, I do." His hand slid across her collarbone and lower before freezing in position. "I thought you were sleeping in clothes this time."

"My dragon's idea." Guilt forged through her because she hadn't precisely argued much. For the sake of peace, she'd taken off her T-shirt.

"Do you do everything your dragon tells you?" Max's thumb worked back and forth over the skin just below her shoulder.

Sasha's breath caught, and everything in her tightened with sensual tension.

"Sasha?"

"My dragon wants me to seduce you and hopefully become pregnant, so you'll keep us with you all the time," Sasha blurted.

This wasn't possible because she'd started taking a contraceptive potion when she broke her fast each morning. She still wasn't certain what had made her do this, and she'd fibbed to her dragon, telling her the potion was part of a new health regime.

The thumb ceased stroking for an instant before it resumed, increasing the crazing-inducing stupor in Sasha.

"Can dragons have offspring with humans?" Max asked.

Sasha wasn't one hundred percent certain and said so. "I don't know, but we are sexually compatible. I mean, our parts will fit. The kissing books and Justine, The Smart Computer, confirmed that."

"Good to know," Max said. "I didn't think to bring condoms with me. An oversight, considering."

"Why?" her dragon demanded. *"Ask him why."*

"My dragon wants to know why this is an oversight," Sasha said.

"Because I've wanted you from the moment I first saw you with Noel. That attraction has increased during the time you've looked after my brother. That Noel likes you, too, increases my feeling for you. Women in my past have rejected my brother because he's different. You get bonus points because you're you, but trapping a man isn't the way to start a happy relationship."

"I know that," Sasha said. "I was about to explain that to my dragon."

"Also, if you became pregnant and traveled home, taking me with you, how would your parents and brothers react? They'd blame me and maybe accuse me of taking advantage of you."

Her dragon sniffed, but Sasha knew Max's words had reached her, and she'd cease pushing that angle.

"However," Max said. "If you and your dragon agree with me, that would be different. We'd be on the same page."

"Describe the page," her dragon ordered.

"What do you mean?" Sasha asked.

"Instead of dancing around the subject, let's make everything clear," Max said. "I want you, and since your dragon is a package deal, that means both of you. I'll be honest, we haven't known each other for long, but I care for you, and what I feel is damn close to love. It wouldn't take much more to push me over the line. Things would be easier if you weren't a lost dragon, but strangely, the complication just makes you more interesting to me."

"You have complications in your life too."

Max brushed a lock of hair away from her face and sought her lips. He brushed a kiss over her mouth. "I have Noel to look after and my grandmother gunning for me. I have no job now that I refuse to return to the one my grandmother maneuvered me into accepting. Talk about manipulation."

"Challenges help us grow," her dragon said, spouting their father's favorite words.

Sasha breathed out a laugh, seeing the incongruity of the memory. "My dragon is pointing out challenges strengthen us."

"Exactly," Max said. "And for the record, I could see a child in our future, but I'd like our lives settled before we move in that direction. Do you agree?"

"Yes," Sasha said.

"We can still have fun and enjoy ourselves until we can get some condoms," Max said.

"We can do anything we want," Sasha said. "The reason I have been taking a draft to prevent a child."

"You didn't tell me," her dragon screeched.

Sasha clapped her hands over her ears until the ringing in her head ceased.

"What's wrong?" Max asked, concern in his features as he pried her fingers away from her ears.

Sasha rolled over to face him properly, her vision perfect in the dark. "I didn't share that information with my dragon. She thought we were taking the potion for the health benefits."

Max laughed. "I see." His expression sobered. "We can still mess around instead of going all the way. I never want you to feel pressured."

"Like you, my interest was snagged as soon as we arrived at your house with Noel. You've been kind to us. Generous."

Max started to speak, and she placed her fingers across his mouth in a signal for him to listen.

"Still my turn," she said with a smile. "The more I've learned about you from your actions, from Noel, and from your grandmother, the more I've liked you. My feelings for you are strong, and if my parents plucked me away from here in five minutes and the barrier came down between us so we could never meet again, I would mourn you."

"God, Sasha." Max's arms came around her, and he hauled her close. "I like the way you say what you think without playing the angles or making everything into a game."

"Apart from not telling you about my dragon."

"Trust takes time to build. I understand that. Keeping your dragon secret was to maintain your safety. You needed to blend with the rest of us. I understand that. Later, you can tell me more about your world, but right now, we have time alone. You're not wearing clothes, despite promising me you would."

"Is he gonna spank us?" her dragon asked.

"Stop! I need to concentrate. I let you drive us when we're flying. Let me take care of this part," Sasha pleaded, barely holding back her groan of frustration. *"Please, I promise we can discuss this to the* nth *degree later. For now, remain quiet, Okay?"*

"But—"

"Please," Sasha said aloud with more than a touch of irritability.

"What's wrong?"

"My dragon is inserting her opinion. I've asked her to hold her questions until later, but she's very opinionated."

"Ah," Max said, his teeth flashing white in the bedroom's darkness. "I have a cure for that. How about if I keep you too busy to think? Would that help?"

"He can do that?" her dragon asked, and she sounded intrigued. *"Tell him to prove it."*

"Yes," Sasha said with a trace of desperation.

Max's rich chortle drove the tension from her stiff shoulders. In the next instant, his lips covered hers. This time it wasn't a gentle kiss. It wasn't a playful kiss. It wasn't a quick kiss. His was a claiming and of the type a male gave a female he adored. At least according to the kissing books she and her dragon had devoured.

Max rose over her and pressed her into the mattress, holding her in place with his bulk. For a man who spent his time sitting at a desk, he had impressive muscles.

She wanted to ask but decided to enjoy and act in the same manner she'd requested of her dragon. Hold all questions until later.

Max kissed her again and slid his tongue across the seam of her lips. She gasped, and he took immediate advantage, exploring the interior of her mouth. *Ooh.* She and her dragon had discussed this French kissing thing, and it wasn't disgusting at all. Every part of her body softened, and she felt his touch clear to her toes. A moan vibrated between them, and she realized the sound came from her.

"Like that, do you?" Max whispered.

"I thought it'd be gross, but I enjoyed it immensely."

Max barked out a laugh. "Excellent. I can't wait for your reaction to the other stuff." He stilled for an instant, his beautiful blue gaze turning somber. "Are you sure you want this? We can't take it back later."

"I've never been more certain of anything in my life." Sasha pulled down his head and kissed him. It lacked finesse, and she decided she needed more practice, but he didn't laugh. Instead, he groaned, and his arms tightened around her. Their tongues slid together in a sensual dance, and excitement pounded through Sasha. Every part of her sizzled with enjoyment, her body light and full of tingling joy. When Max parted their mouths, her breath caught because she was eager to learn what would happen next.

When the suspense became too much for her, she exclaimed, "What's next?"

"That's what I want to know," her dragon said. *"So far, it has been enlightening and immensely enjoyable."*

"Shush," Sasha reminded her dragon.

Max chuckled. "This is the most interesting time I've ever had in bed with a woman."

"Only interesting?" Her dragon sounded disappointed, and Sasha echoed the emotion.

"Is that bad?"

"Hell, no," Max said immediately. He hesitated as if he wanted to say something but thought the better of it.

"Honesty is always best," she reminded him. "I prefer it."

"I do, too," Max said. "Do you know what happens? Did your mother tell you?"

"My mother would've told me before my betrothal became

official, although my friend shared what her mother told her recently before my friend's marriage."

"All right."

"Her mother didn't tell her much. I hope my mother was intending to tell me more. I've picked up a little by eavesdropping on my older brothers, but I've learned the most during my time on the mainland. My dragon and I read lots of kissing books, and when we didn't understand something, we asked Justine, The Smart Computer."

"I see."

Max bore a weird expression as if he wanted to laugh but was frightened of hurting her feelings. The knowledge warmed her through.

"We watched some stuff that Justine showed us on the internet. There was lots of grunting and groaning and a woman wailing about a big dick."

"You watched porn?"

"I think that is what they called it."

"Oh," Max said, biting his lip again while mirth danced in his blue, blue eyes. "All right then. No more talking. Just feeling, okay."

"Tell him to hurry," her dragon said. *"We grow older while we wait."*

Sasha burst out laughing.

"What?"

"I promise to tell you later." She aimed a kiss at his lips and got his chin instead. It was faintly prickly beneath her mouth and tongue. Fascinated, she raised her fingers to explore the roughness.

"You have my permission to touch me anywhere you like. Anything you enjoy me doing to you, I'll probably get the same pleasure from too."

Emboldened, she ran her fingers down his neck. She kissed the strong column and tasted a faint saltiness. Recalling one of her kissing books, she sucked slightly, and he rewarded her with a masculine groan. Sasha let her fingers wander his collarbone and lower, his firm chest. She kissed and sucked and explored, elated when Max's breathing became hoarse.

She lifted the blankets. "That looks painful."

Max grunted. "It's not. My erection is a physical reaction to your presence. Your touch. Your kisses. Your scent."

"Can I remove the last of your clothes?"

"Not now," Max said in a hoarse voice. "We'll leave that until later. How about I explore you for a while?"

"Okay. What should I do?"

Max's eyes crinkled in silent humor. "You can touch me in return if you want, otherwise enjoy. If I do anything you're not sure of, tell me to stop. Okay?"

"Yes."

Eager anticipation pulsed to life in her. At long last, they'd get to experience more of the things they'd learned from the kissing books.

Max started slowly. He caressed her mouth and slipped his tongue between her lips. Just as she opened her mouth to complain of the repetition, his hands wandered down her arm to stroke the slightly rougher skin where her dragon lay on her torso. Her dragon's purr rippled through her mind, but Sasha got the feeling Max could do much more. Seconds later, he proved her right when his hand settled on her breast. A double whammy since his touch had her dragon purring louder while the brush of his fingers against her nipple had darts surging down her torso to collect between her thighs.

"You're so pretty," Max murmured. "Inside and out. And you're soft, but I can feel the muscles beneath your skin. You're sleek and sexy."

"Thank you. I like your body too."

Max's eyes crinkled again, and he resettled his torso. Instead of using his fingers to shape her breast and tease her nipple, he sucked the peak into his mouth.

She gasped, and when he would've moved, she held him in place. He chuckled and teased her other breast while he used his mouth to excellent effect, driving every thought from her head. Meanwhile, her dragon continued to purr and seemed incapable of adding any comments now that Max had rubbed her belly.

Max's hands skimmed lower until he reached her upper thigh. His warm touch seemed to brand her skin, and a shiver rolled over her. Strangely, every touch and every sensation curled together in a ball at the place between her legs. She gasped as he puffed his warm breath over her sex.

Moisture had gathered there, and if she hadn't known better, she might have wondered if she was sickening for something. But no, her body was working perfectly. Max skimmed a finger over her flesh, and she jolted at the frisson of pleasure.

"I'm glad you know what to do," she whispered.

He laughed before asking, "Does that bother you?"

"No, one of us has to direct this operation. Besides, you're sharing your experience with me, and your knowledge is making me happy. You seem to know exactly where to touch me."

"Good to know," Max said. "Last chance to change your mind."

"Not happening." Confidence and certainty rang in her tone.

Max's smile turned blinding white, and the emotion in his face pushed her heart to beat harder. Faster. "In that case," he whispered, "Let me taste you."

He replaced his finger with the softness of his tongue, and he lapped at her juices.

"Ooh!" Sasha said and gripped the bedclothes.

"Should I stop?"

"No! No, don't stop."

Her stomach clenched, and her grip on the bedclothes tightened. The pleasure was slow and rolled through her in a gentle wave. Instinctively, her hips arched upward to get Max to increase the pressure. Max chuckled and continued to stroke her with both fingers and mouth until she buzzed and yearned for something extra. He traced her opening in a teasing, maddening stroke when she ached for a mysterious more.

He pushed his finger deeper, and it slipped inside her, the intrusion welcoming and stimulating, yet still not enough.

"Max," she wailed.

He chuckled softly, yet it wasn't cruel humor. It was more knowing. Teasing. Yep, still maddening. His finger crooked inside her, and he teased an inner wall while his tongue massaged her happy spot.

Immediately, the pleasure within her darted higher, going so fast she became breathless. She gasped, swallowed hard, frightened to move for fear of losing this wondrous stimulation. But she needn't have worried. Instead, the sensations expanded until it felt as if she balanced on a precipice of pleasure and pain. A part of her wanted Max to stop, and the other side of her was frightened he would cease giving her this gift.

Without warning, Max suckled harder, and she was flying, her body squeezing Max's fingers. She thought she might've cried out and couldn't find enough energy to care. Wow. Just wow. She'd been missing out all this time.

Max withdrew his finger, and her sex gave a protesting twitch as if the emptiness was a punishment. He rose up her body, pausing to pinch her nipple. Yet another spasm resulted from the streak of pain.

She was about to ask questions, but Max's mouth covered hers, and he kissed her slowly and thoroughly. Their tongues danced together. She could taste herself on his lips and savored his unique smoky flavor in return.

His groin brushed against her hip, which propelled another surge of want to life. She parted their lips and ran her fingers over his bristly jawline.

"Do I get to see you with no clothes?"

"Yeah."

He pulled away and slid off the bed. Seconds later, he was naked.

"That looks even more painful," her dragon said.

"Can I touch it?"

"Not right now," he said. "You're hell on my restraint. Just the thought of having your hands roving my body is enough to make me burst. How about this first time, we move straight along? I promise, hand on my heart, you can explore as much as you want next time."

"All right," Sasha said.

"Great," Max said before he kissed her again.

Her dragon's moan rumbled through Sasha's head. *"I love kissing Max,"* her dragon whispered.

"Radio silence, remember. Like they did in that movie we watched last week."

"Radio silence," her dragon confirmed and kept her promise by

not doing anything more than purr her happiness.

Max dragged Sasha over him then stroked his hand down her back and over her buttocks. Every one of his touches brought new shivers of delight and more beautiful memories to drag out later. He squeezed her arse and drew her against him, so their bodies fit together perfectly. His cock slipped between her thighs, sliding across tender flesh and setting off another series of delightful prickles. No matter where he touched, her body surged at the caress. Her nerves pulsated, sending never-ending darts of pleasure swimming through her mind.

"This might hurt the first time," Max warned as he twisted their bodies again until she lay flat on the mattress. He settled between her legs, his expression grave.

"I know," she said. "I'm ready. Besides, I doubt it will hurt for long. Dragons heal fast."

Max kissed her chin, the tip of her nose, and nuzzled at her neck. "All you need to do is tell me to stop."

"I won't."

"Fast or slow?"

Sasha groaned. "Do I have to tell you to stop talking?"

His chuckle filled the air even as he fitted his cock to her flesh and pushed inside her. Her nails dug into his back, her hiss of surprise hidden against his shoulder. There was a hint of pain—yes—but it wasn't as bad as she'd expected. Instead, she felt an incredible sense of fullness, and she guessed there would be more and better to come.

Max pulled back, reducing the pressure inside her. For one awful moment, she thought he'd halt, but he silenced her complaints with his mouth and surged inside her again.

Sasha groaned as a fleeting tease of bliss streaked through her veins. Instinctively, she lifted her hips, seeking more of the sensation. Max made a sound, too, and quickened the pace of his strokes into her body. She clung to him, the pain a distant memory. Instead, she focused on grabbing the beautiful pulses that came from their joining. Pleasure grew, and it was even better than earlier because she was sharing the moment with Max. She clutched his shoulders and undulated with him.

"Sasha," he murmured. "Kiss me."

"Anytime. Always."

Their lips met, yet Max kept thrusting into her body, driving her mindless. This was so much better than her imagination. So much better.

"Sweetheart, I wanted this to last longer." He gasped out the words as his hips jerked, and his thrusts grew harder and faster.

Sasha didn't care since she was right there with him. She held on for dear life and enjoyed the heck out of their physical journey.

Max reached between them and stroked her nub. Seconds later, she shattered, and he groaned. The pleasure roared through her, stealing her breath, her sight, and emptying her mind of everything except Max.

His hips worked in two fast thrusts before he stilled, and her channel pulsed around him again. A loud click sounded inside her head, and she groaned, tipsy from the extraordinary experience.

Long moments later, her dragon said, *"What was that weird click? Did we break?"*

Sasha sighed. *"Don't know about you, but I'm feeling no pain. That was incredible."*

"Thank you," Max said. *"It was amazing."* He stiffened. *"You didn't speak aloud."* He parted their bodies, and Sasha mourned the loss of the intimate contact. *"Why can I hear you?"*

"What?" Sasha whispered, staring at him. She imagined the shock on his face echoed hers.

"Woohoo!" her dragon cheered.

"Why are you woohooing?" Max asked.

He sounded a little freaked, and Sasha babbled, "That's my dragon half. I never believed the old tales my grandfather told us about some dragons having true mates."

"But—" Max started.

"Shush," her dragon said. *"Listen to Sasha. She will explain."*

CHAPTER 12

Love and True Mates

M ax rolled onto his back, his body sated by the most fantastic sex he'd had in living memory. He hesitated then decided he should give in to his urge to take Sasha into his arms. He could listen to Sasha while he savored her warm body next to his. Her touch quelled the flash of panic that had seized him on hearing the strange feminine voice in his head. Sasha had done nothing to harm either him or Noel. He'd made love to her, so it was up to him to offer the gift of trust. He'd listen to her explanation.

Max cleared his throat. "Go on," he said.

"My grandfather told me some dragons in the past had found their true mates, and this meant they could communicate on a private channel. When I'm in my dragon form, I can communicate with other dragons, but now we have a means of speaking together without other dragons overhearing."

"That was your dragon?"

He felt the curve of Sasha's smile against his shoulder rather than saw it. "It was my dragon. I scarcely believe it myself, but we are true mates."

"The stuff of legends," her dragon trilled, sounding excited.

Max fell silent, trying to analyze how he felt about this. Aw, hell. Who was he trying to kid? He'd fallen for Sasha in a big way. Yes, she was younger, but she was so special. On top of that, she was gorgeous, and her broad grin, her sense of fun, and her ability to make Noel happy pleased him too.

"Are you going to say something? Anything?" her dragon snapped finally.

"I'm pleased to meet you. This is a lot to get my head around. I am but a male, and I require time to assess everything." He thought the words rather than stating them aloud, then held his breath for a reaction.

"Well said," the dragon replied after a long beat of silence. *"What will we do next? You're connected to Sasha and me now. I knew you were perfect for us. I told Sasha."*

Sasha shifted a fraction in his arms, her shoulders shaking in silent merriment.

"Why are you laughing?" Sasha's dragon demanded.

"I want to know that, too," Max said aloud.

"You sound like our mother with the smug I-told-you-so. The last time when we were together at the family dinner, our mother told-us-so about something, and you grumbled and growled for hours."

"*Ooh,*" Sasha's dragon whispered, and she sounded a bit bemused. "*That's bad. Does sex do something weird to your brain? Should Justine, The Smart Computer, have warned us about that?*"

Max barked out a laugh. "No, you're fine in the sex department. No side effects apart from pleasure plus a mate bond. The I-told-you-so is all you."

"*Dang,*" Sasha's dragon said. "*Gotta fix that. Kiss us and make us forget.*"

"Now that I can do," Max murmured, and he set about making them all forget everything except the pleasure of intimacy and touch.

Many hours later, Noel stirred in the next door bedroom, his thumps drawing their attention.

"Noel is awake," Sasha said, starting to slip from the bed.

"Stay," Max said. "Take a shower and come out when you're ready. I'll start Noel on cereal and make us a pot of tea." He snatched a quick kiss and strode toward the connected bathroom.

"*He has a very nice arse,*" Sasha's dragon said. "*I want to bite it. Do you think Max would like that?*"

Sasha's dragon had forgotten he could eavesdrop on this

particular channel.

Max chuckled. *"As long as it isn't with your sharp dragon teeth, I might enjoy a bite or two."* He closed the bathroom door and took care of business while listening to the conversation in his mind. *"Can I turn off the chatter if I want?"* he asked silently.

"All you have to do is ask me," Sasha's dragon said snootily. *"I can switch to just Sasha. You're new, and I forgot."*

"I didn't mean to offend you. This is new to me too. It will take time for us to adjust," Max replied.

"True," Sasha's dragon said. *"I would change nothing. I like you very much."*

"Thank you," Max said. *"I like you very much. You're gorgeous."*

"There!" Sasha's dragon shrieked. *"Proof of what I've been saying all along. We're gorgeous, and Max would be a fool if he walked away from us."*

Max stiffened. *"You're frightened that I'm going to have passionate sex—the best sex of my life—and just walk off into the sunset?"*

"No," Sasha said forcefully. *"That is not what we're worried about, although leaving wouldn't be very nice of you. We're worried about the barrier and the fact we come from different worlds."*

"That's fair. You sensed the barrier during the flight here, right?" Max finished in the bathroom and returned to the bedroom to grab a pair of swim shorts and a T-shirt.

Sasha's dragon gave a loud sigh as he tugged down the shirt

to hide his chest. He winked at Sasha while he waited for her to answer.

"Yes, the barrier seems intact. I felt a reluctance to go too near it, which must be what the humans feel on this side. I guess the *dread* keeps away the fishermen while the big ships that travel the coast don't come this far north."

"All right," Max said. "Once we've had breakfast, we'll go for a walk. If we stroll toward the end of the island, we should avoid most of the tourists. From memory, they hang around the town to visit the abbey or the castle before they head back across the causeway."

"Sounds like a plan," Sasha said.

"Max!" Noel screeched.

"Shower," Max said firmly. "You're probably a bit sore, and the warm water will ease your muscles."

"Max! Shasha!"

Max opened the bedroom door. "In here, buddy. Are you hungry?"

"I couldn't find you," Noel sobbed.

"We're right here. Let's get you washed and dressed, then we'll make Sasha breakfast."

"Shasha makes breakfast," Noel said, leaning into Max's legs. A wave of love for his little brother filled him. No way was he letting his grandmother take custody. No matter what, even if he had to break the law to do it.

"Today, we'll make breakfast for a change to give Sasha a rest." Max's mind busily worked through his options as he washed Noel's face and helped him to comb his hair. His conclusion—his decision depended on Sasha because he loathed the idea of walking away from her. Besides, he suspected this mate bond ran both ways. Throughout the morning, he'd experienced a sense of well-being and happiness that echoed his own. It was weird that he felt it in his gut, and he could sense Sasha's presence before she fully entered the room. To test himself, he said, "Tea?"

"Please," Sasha said as she strode into the dining area.

"Shasha," Noel said, and his round face was one big beam.

"Noel's behavior has been so much better since you came into our lives." Max sent the thought to Sasha. When he placed the mug of tea in front of her, she squeezed his forearm.

"Thank you," she said.

Max checked on the bacon and cracked three eggs into the pan. He placed four slices of bread into the toaster, checked the darkness setting, and popped it down to cook. "What did you do on Perfume Isle? Did you have a job?"

"No. Most of my friends were the same. We stay at home until our parents arrange a betrothal, and then we move to join our new husband." She pursed her lips, her discontent shining through. "That's part of the problem in our world. Dragons my age—the women—have no occupation apart from running the home and looking after their families. Looking after Noel for you was fun, yet it gave me a sense of self-worth too. It's the first time I've ever earned money and purchased things I wanted. If I went home, it'd be difficult to settle again. Maybe I could talk to my parents and try to explain, but I doubt they'd understand. My brothers are lucky. They have more freedom."

"What would you do if you had the opportunity?"

"I love looking after Noel and helping him learn new things. Maybe I could be a teacher."

"Don't you have schools in your world?"

"The boys have tutors and university. Some women go, but they're usually from wealthy families. My mother taught me to cook and run a household, how to do needlework, and conduct myself in public and at parties. That sort of thing."

"You're too intelligent to waste your skills on running a home. Not that that isn't an important job, but you require a challenge." Max served the bacon and eggs and rescued the toast.

Soon, they were all eating.

"Noel, would you like to walk after breakfast?" Max asked.

"Beach," Noel said immediately. "Swim."

"We could manage that," Max said.

An hour later, they set off for a walk. Although it was still early—just after nine—the sun was shining, and it promised to be a hot day. Not a cloud marred the blue sky. They exited a white wooden gate at the rear of the property, and a few minutes later, they were on the beach.

"I didn't realize we were that close," Sasha said. "Last night, I was too busy watching for danger."

"Well, this is handy since it will keep Noel happy." Max glanced along the beach, and on seeing no one, he asked, "Can you sense the barrier?"

He'd noticed her distracted air and sensed she was gauging her surroundings. It must be disconcerting to find oneself in another land. Pride swept through him. Sasha had coped admirably with all the changes tossed at her. He didn't think he would've done as well under the same circumstances.

Sasha grabbed his arm, excitement blazing across her face. "The barrier is down. When we first came outside, I sensed it, but the faint buzz it emits has ceased." She took two steps before releasing a heartfelt groan. "It's back again."

Max hated her disappointment because he knew she missed her family. "Let's walk along the beach. We'll go that way, so we're wandering away from the castle. It's best if we stay away from the town because Noel stands out with his Down syndrome. If I end up not returning to Bamburgh, we don't want to leave a trail of clues."

"*Plan,*" Sasha's dragon whispered. "*I love to explore unfamiliar places.*"

"Aren't you worried about not flying as often and not seeing your parents?" Max asked, his curiosity rising. Sasha was such a complex woman with her dual personalities. He'd have thought she and her dragon would be more similar, but her dragon half seemed more impulsive and quick to temper. Yet her quips and smart-arse comments amused the heck out of him.

"Sasha and I both miss our parents," the dragon said. *"But we're happy with our adventure too. They protected us and forbade anything fun."*

"It's a parents' job to protect their children. I worry about Noel," Max said.

"They need to learn balance and stop trying to marry us off to Bruceous," the dragon snapped. *"Who is that?"*

Max pivoted in the direction Sasha gestured. "It looks like a child and two women."

"What do you want to do?" Sasha asked. "I can investigate the barrier once night falls again."

"They've seen us. The kid is waving. If we turn around now, it's going to seem strange. They're more likely to remember our rudeness," Max said.

"Okay, so we continue our meander along the beach, exchange pleasantries, and go on our way," Sasha said. "Noel, look at the shells over there. Let's see if they're different from the ones we collected at home."

Max drifted after Sasha, dividing his attention between Noel and Sasha and the two women. One had bright red hair while the other had brown.

Although they watched the child closely, they constantly

chattered, their laughter floating through the air. Perhaps they'd pass each other without them getting a close look at Noel.

At that moment, Noel spotted the other child and beelined toward them. Well, there went that faint possibility. Let's hope the child wasn't an obnoxious twat who'd comment on Noel's differences. Max took long strides to catch up with Sasha and Noel. By the time he reached them, the two children were busy discussing the shells Noel had collected.

"Max," Sasha spoke through their mind link. *"I can smell dragon on the child, but they're humans."*

"Hello," a friendly voice said. "I see you've met my daughter."

"I'm a boy today," the girl shouted.

The brown-haired woman rolled her eyes. "Joanna, it's rude to shout in front of strangers."

"But this is Noel," Joanna said. "He told me, so he's not a stranger."

The redhead chuckled. "You can't fault the logic. Are you here for a holiday? We're staying in a cottage not far from here."

"Yes," Max said. "Work has been stressful lately, and we wanted to take a break from the bustle on the mainland."

"I get that," the brown-haired woman said. "We'll let you get on with your walk. Maybe we'll see you around again."

Max forced a smile. "Noel loves to walk on the beach."

"Joanna does too. I figure if she races around and uses up her excess energy, she'll sleep better. Nice to meet you." She shepherded her daughter along and continued walking with her friend while he and Sasha stared after them.

Their first helpful clue.

CHAPTER 13

Mysterious Humans and a Reunion

S asha swallowed her shout of glee as she glanced over her shoulder at the retreating women and child. The women had smelled strongly of dragons, even though both were human. Sudden tightness in her chest had her pressing her hand to her breastbone and counteracting her initial excitement. Friend or foe?

"Max," she murmured. "The women bore the scent of dragons too." She hesitated then decided keeping the details from Max was silly after the intimacy between them. "My guess is they've had sex with a dragon. Different dragons," she added when Max's eyebrows rose. "Each of them has a dragon lover."

Max reached for her and drew her closer. "What do you want to do?"

"I should be able to follow their tracks later and trail them back to where the women are staying. If I observe in secret, I might learn more or at least spot another dragon."

"You're not going alone," Max said.

"I'll be perfectly safe."

"Yes, you're strong and clever and can fly, but you've mentioned male dragons. It'd be two against one."

Sasha understood his fear. "That's why I want to sneak around."

"Better idea," Max said. "Why don't we go in the direction they've come from now? With humans around and broad daylight, any dragon is going to think twice about shifting. It should be safer. In theory."

Sasha considered Max's idea. "All right. We'll stroll, and if I sense danger of any kind, we'll retreat."

"Works for me. The barrier is still present, right?" Max asked.

"Yes, it's working."

"Do I smell like a dragon now?"

Sasha's eyes widened, and she leaned close enough to sniff his neck. She licked his skin, something she'd never have dared before. She or her dragon might have considered the idea, but Sasha was sure they would've rejected it immediately. Now, she did it because she could. At the same time, she inhaled. Max's essence filled her lungs, along with a hint of her.

"Yep, you smell like you made love with a dragon," her dragon informed Max. *"Me."*

Max burst into laughter. "I'll grab Noel. You start your tracking thing, and we'll catch up."

"I'm terrified," Sasha confessed.

"Me too," Max said. "I don't want to lose you."

"Even though we're different?"

"It's your differences that make you stand out, that make you special to me," Max said. Sincerity and truth rang in his words.

Sasha jumped, and he caught her in his arms and spun them around. She was breathless and laughing by the time he kissed her. He parted their lips and released her with a pat on the bottom.

"We should hustle. You'll want to do your tracking before the women decide to return to their cottage."

"Yes," Sasha agreed, her emotions more level now that Max had kissed the life out of her. "I'll go slowly."

She followed the footprints in the sand while scanning the beach in front of them. Max was as quick as he promised and soon caught up with her.

"Where we go, Shasha?"

"I'm showing Max how to follow a trail," she said.

"Like you did when I was lost," Noel said.

"That's right, buddy," Max said. "But we need to be quiet so Sasha can concentrate on tracking. Okay?"

Noel fell silent, and Sasha increased her speed, the tracks easy to follow. Soon, the trail headed up the beach toward a grassy bank. Sasha slowed, casting out her senses because the dragon scent was more pungent here.

"*You okay?*" Max asked through their mate bond.

"*Still scared,*" Sasha said. "*Nervous about what I might find.*"

"*I'm here with you. The women were friendly and didn't give off bad vibes. Their dragon lovers must treat them well, which leads me to think they should be okay.*"

"*Maybe,*" Sasha said, but the apprehension inside her increased. She'd feel better if the dragon scent was a familiar one, but these were strangers. They might attack first and ask questions later. She'd never forgive herself if Max, or worse Noel, became injured because she'd wanted to find her way home.

"*We don't even know if we want to go home,*" her dragon said on their private channel. "*I mean, what will our parents do, and what happened to the arrangement with Bruceous? We're mated with Max. Becoming forcibly parted from him won't do us any good, and it will hurt Max and Noel, too.*"

"*I know. This is so hard. I'm torn, and it's a horrid feeling.*"

Max placed a hand on her shoulder. "*Keep going, Sasha. No matter what, I'm here at your side. We do this together.*"

Sasha swallowed hard. This grown-up business was tough. Justine, The Smart Computer, had made it seem effortless when she'd directed them to relevant sources. "Okay," she murmured.

"The scent goes to the wooden gate over there. I'll creep closer and peer through the fence."

"I'll be right behind you," Max promised as he gave her shoulder an encouraging squeeze.

Sasha crept closer. The low rumble of masculine voices came to her, and she quickly checked on the wind direction. Thankfully, the breeze was blowing her way. Luck was with her this once. With her gaze on the garden beyond the fence, she failed to see a piece of driftwood. When she planted her foot on the stick, a sharp crack broke the silence. She froze in alarm. Holy f-bombs.

The male chatter ceased, and her stomach fluttered with nerves. What if they came to see who was out here? Or if the women returned? Her pulse raced, and sweat gathered on her brow. With caution, she lifted her foot and winced at her close call. They hadn't come to investigate. She edged farther along the fence to get a better look at the people socializing in the garden. Max followed, and when she spared him a glance, she noted he was taking care of his footfalls.

"Did you want something?" a masculine voice drawled.

A second male voice said, "Are you spying on us?"

Sasha cursed under her breath and slowly raised her gaze to study the two massive dragon males observing her and Max with clear suspicion.

"You had to stand on a stick," her dragon groused.

"Do you recognize them?" Max asked.

"No," Sasha said.

"Hello," a feminine voice said from behind them before Sasha had decided what to tell the dragons.

"We thought this was a public walkway," Sasha said. "So sorry. We'll be going."

"Don't be silly," the brown-haired woman said. "Stay for a cup of tea. Joanna would love to have someone to play with."

"Thank you," Max said. "We'd love to have tea." He and Sasha moved out of the way of the women.

The girl ran straight to Noel. "Do you like to draw pictures? I draw dragons. Can you draw a dragon?"

"I flew on a dragon," Noel said in a clear voice.

"Did you?" the redhead said without a blink. "That must've been something."

"I hate to bother you," Sasha said.

"Come in. Have tea. Tell us why you're skulking at our gate," one man said, his gaze sharp. Suspicious.

Before Sasha knew it, the two women had ushered them into the enclosed garden area. Noel ran to the deck area with the girl.

"I think introductions are in order," the brown-haired woman said. "I'm Liza. That's my daughter Joanna over there, and this is my mate, Leo." She gestured at the closest man who had long black hair and piercing green eyes.

"I'm Cherry," the redhead said then pointed at the second male who had black curly hair. "Martinos. Also, my mate."

Both women glanced at Sasha and Max expectantly. Sasha hesitated, apprehension rippling through her to settle at the pit of her stomach. Now that she'd found actual dragons, she worried about Max's and Noel's safety. *Her* safety.

"There you are," another masculine voice called.

Sasha frowned and turned toward the new arrival. One glimpse of the familiar face, and she was running, her feet flying across the grass. She flung herself at her brother. "Blaze! You're here."

"Sasha." Shock filled her oldest brother's expression, but he beamed at her, and his beefy arms wrapped around her and held tight. "I've been so worried about you. I can't believe you're here. Safe. I was about to start a search here and on the mainland."

Sasha squeezed her brother again before pulling back. "Blaze, I want you to meet someone." She turned to Max and offered a reassuring smile even though nerves continued to tap-dance through her. "This is Max. He's my mate."

Blaze tensed for a moment before arching a brow in her direction. "Your mate?"

"Yes," Sasha said, lifting her chin. "I love him."

"Are you positive?"

"I've learned grandmother's tales of soulmates are true," she said, her tone fierce.

"Okay." Blaze hesitated before he offered his hand to Max in the human way. Sasha hadn't even known Blaze knew of the custom. "My sister looks happy, but if you ever hurt her, you'll have me to

231

deal with."

"Why would I hurt her?" Max demanded. "I love her."

"Knock it off, Blaze," Sasha said, her eyes narrowing. "Max won't hurt me."

"Shasha! Shasha!" Noel came running up to her. "Joanna can draw dragons."

Sasha smiled at Noel. "That's excellent. She can teach you something new."

Noel nodded.

"This is Blaze. He's my brother," she said.

"Max has a kid," Blaze said, his gaze narrowed. His nostrils flared, and his scowl grew deeper. "He smells like you."

"I told you Max is my mate," Sasha snapped. "We both look after Noel, so he has our scents. Get this into your head. Max is mine, and I'm his. We are mates, and nothing you do will separate us. It would be cruel even to try because the mating bonds have snapped into place. We speak over our own channel."

"Everything Sasha says is true. I love Sasha, and she is my mate." Max glanced at Noel, the tension in him as great as her brother's. "Noel is my little brother, not my son," Max said. "My parents died a few months ago, and I have responsibility for Noel."

"The tea is ready," Liza called. "Come and join us."

"Are you a dragon?" Noel asked Blaze.

Blaze's shoulders relaxed. He flashed a grin at Noel, and the tension bled from Sasha as her brother crouched in front of Noel.

"I am a dragon."

Noel patted Blaze's arm. "I like dragons." He trotted off to join Joanna again.

Sasha trailed Noel, walking between Max and Blaze. Tension still simmered in her brother, and she sensed he needed to observe Max before he fully accepted she had a mate. At least, he was withholding judgment for now.

"Where have you been?" Blaze asked. "We've searched for you everywhere. Once we learned Leo flew through the barrier and met Liza, our hope grew. We knew you'd been flying. It's taken us time to arrange travel to this side of the barrier."

"I'm sorry I worried everyone. My dragon flew into the thick air before we realized what had happened, and then it was too late. We landed on the beach to reconnoiter and discovered Noel. We had to help him because it was dark, and he was a child alone. Later, Max offered me a job," Sasha said. "I've been checking the barrier, but it always seemed intact. I couldn't get home. Are Mother and Father all right? They can't make me go ahead with the betrothal to Bruceous. Max truly is my mate. We mind speak."

"You had sex with my sister," Blaze said on a growl.

"Blaze. Quit that. We're mates. Sex is part of the deal," Sasha snapped.

"*Yeah!*" her dragon echoed, and she climbed higher on Sasha's body to glare at their brother.

"I did because I love her like crazy," Max said firmly. "And she loves me in return. We're together, and that's final."

"Excellent answer," Blaze said, tension leaching from his shoulders. "I'm your big brother and your only family here. I take this responsibility seriously."

"Max helps to keep us safe," Sasha's dragon said with yet another glower at her brother.

"Will you side with me if Mother and Father disagree with my decision?" Sasha asked.

"I don't know yet. Wait until I know Max better," Blaze said.

"Hurry," Leo called. "Otherwise, Joanna and Noel will eat the cake. You'll miss out."

"This is your missing sister?" Cherry asked when they finally joined the others.

"Yes," Blaze said. "Your timing is excellent, Sasha, since I was about to travel to the mainland to begin my search for you."

"You're truly here to look for me?" Sasha asked.

"Griffith is arriving later tonight. He was going to help. Come and tell us again what happened and what you did. We'd all like to listen to the story."

"Is it safe to talk in front of the others?" Sasha asked through her private family channel.

"Yes. We're friends here, and we've fought for each other. I bet you our story is better than your adventure."

"Our brother has no idea," Sasha's dragon said.

Sasha rolled her eyes, agreeing with her dragon, and took a seat next to Max.

"Okay?" he murmured.

"I think so."

Once Cherry and Liza distributed the tea and cakes, Sasha related the events that had led to her meeting Noel and Max, and how they'd ended up coming to Holy Island because of Max's grandmother.

"That's terrible," Liza said. "My ex-husband was trying a similar thing with Joanna. It was greed because my father has money, and my ex wanted his share—even though he didn't deserve a thing."

"What will you do now?" Cherry asked. "What if your private investigator doesn't find the info he's looking for in the next two days?"

"I should take Noel and run, preferably to a place the cops will never find him. I'd need to start again and find a job to support Sasha and Noel," Max said. "The last thing I want is to let my grandmother take Noel, especially if she merely wants the money for Noel's support. My brother deserves to have people in his life who love him."

"His Down syndrome doesn't slow him down," Liza said. "Leo, Joanna, and I are returning to the Dragon Isles while Cherry and Martinos are setting up a business in Bamburgh. You could go to Perfume Isle with Blaze and Griffith and live there. Give Cherry and Martinos your friend's contact details and communicate via them."

Blaze indicated agreement. "That's an excellent idea. Noel would be safe. You'd have the opportunity to prove to Mother and Father you're happy and secure with Max. I think they'd like Noel. He'll charm them."

"What sort of job did you do?" Leo asked.

"I was a reporter," Max said.

"Set up a newspaper," Liza said. "Part of the problem with the Dragon Isles is the lack of easy contact between the three islands. A weekly newspaper could help with that. Henry might transport it between the islands for you. At the least, a newspaper would keep every resident apprised of the important news. It might be a way to advertise for people to move to Smoking Isle as well."

"A newspaper is a fantastic idea," Leo said. "I enjoyed reading of the things happening on the mainland when Cherry brought the paper home yesterday."

"I could do that," Max said. "Or try my hand at other work. I don't want anyone to accuse me of freeloading. As long as Noel and Sasha are safe and happy, and we can support ourselves."

"I could write kissing books," Sasha said. "My friends and other dragons—maybe the humans too—might enjoy reading kissing books."

"Kissing books?" Cherry asked with interest.

"Romances," Max said.

"Oh," Cherry said with a wink at Liza. "I think we're going to get along great with Sasha."

"But I can sense the barrier," Sasha said. "How did you get here? How is it possible for you to travel from the Dragon Isles to Holy Island?"

"That," Liza said, "is a very long story. You might have to stay for lunch." She glanced at her mate and her friends. "Should I start by telling Sasha what happened to me?"

Sasha and Max listened as Liza told them her story of what occurred after Leo rescued her from the sea. Cherry took up the tale, and once she'd finished her recitation of how she'd found Martinos on the beach, both women, plus Leo, Martinos, and Blaze, informed them what had happened next and how they'd stopped a group of dragons from taking over the mainland.

"Wow," Max said. "Do the rest of the dragons understand what happened?"

Leo shook his head. "Most of them are clueless. Some wouldn't believe the skullduggery that played out under their noses."

Max's gaze narrowed. "What do you hope will happen now? Will you let everyone know what has happened? How will you stop it from happening again?"

Liza laughed aloud. "You're definitely a reporter."

"Most people on the Dragon Isles can read. I think we *should* publish a basic newspaper here and deliver it to the residents," Cherry said. "We can use a desktop publishing system and print out the copies. Cherry and I can drive over to the mainland and get whatever supplies we need."

"Brilliant idea," Leo said. "It would be faster to get the news out this way. If Max agrees, he could travel back to the monastery and interview David and Rena."

"Who are they?" Sasha asked.

"Rena is my sister," Liza said. "David is her husband. Allen, a minister we know, married them a week ago. They're on their honeymoon, but they'll be back at the monastery tomorrow."

Max turned to Sasha. "What do you think?"

"If you're on one of the Dragon Isles, you and Noel will be out of the reach of your grandparents. Doing the newspaper would allow you to write the type of story you enjoy rather than the tabloid-type stories you hate. And it would give us a chance to visit my parents."

Sasha continued, "As much as I'd like to stay away from them, if I want to prove I'm an adult and capable of looking after myself, I have to front up and tell them why I refuse to obey their order to become betrothed to Bruceous."

Blaze started clapping, his open approval, bringing a grin to her face. "An attitude like that should convince Mother and Father you know what you're doing. I'll go with you and Max in support."

"Thank you," Max said.

"*So we're doing this,*" Sasha said on their private channel. "*Traveling to the monastery while Liza and Cherry organize the equipment for you to print your story.*"

"*We're doing this,*" Max agreed.

CHAPTER 14

Meet The Parents

The next two days were full of work but fun as well. Griffith arrived, and Max liked the youngest of Sasha's brothers. Max interviewed Liza and Leo and also Martinos and Cherry. He wrote their stories and gained their approval once they'd read them.

"You're good," Liza said. "It's perfect. You've set out the facts without embellishments, yet it's an interesting read."

"Can you and Cherry do the layout while I write my additional stories?" Max asked.

"I can," Liza said.

Max shot a glance at the others in the room and leaned toward

Liza. "Do you know Sasha's parents? How do you think they'll react to me?"

"I've met Sasha's mother. She was amazing, feeding us when we turned up unexpectedly. None of Sasha's family—the ones I've met—show a bias toward humans. It's obvious to me you love each other. I think it will be fine since Blaze and Griffith are supporting you."

Max grimaced. "I can't help feeling nervous."

Liza patted his shoulder. "They're much nicer than Leo's family or Martinos's family."

"True. From what you've told me, this should be much easier, but that doesn't stop me worrying."

The next day, they walked to the portal with Blaze. Griffith had already left and would meet them at the monastery. Noel had taken to Blaze as quickly as he'd warmed to Sasha, and Blaze held Noel's hand while Max held Sasha's.

"Is the journey through the portal difficult?" Max asked.

"I don't know," Sasha whispered. "Blaze and the others wouldn't have suggested this if it was dangerous for a child."

The info didn't exactly settle the nerves hopping in Max's gut, and it made him realize Sasha must've faced similar worries when she entered his world. She'd managed so well he and others she'd met hadn't sensed her dragon. Yes, she'd appeared slightly foreign, but she'd thrown herself at the challenge without hesitation.

He must behave in the same way.

With that thought fixed in his mind, he straightened and grinned at Sasha. "Let's do this."

Blaze showed them to a grove of trees. Yew trees. Max recalled from his time at school and his history studies how vital these trees had been to his forbears. He'd read the trees held magical properties.

In the center of the grove, the air blurred and churned at a point in front of them.

"This is it," Blaze said. "Just step into that spot. Noel and I will go first." He lifted Noel into his arms, making Max's brother chortle in delight. In the next instant, they'd both disappeared.

"Our turn," Max said.

"Are you sure about this? I'm uncertain of how my parents will react."

"Blaze is on our side, now that he knows me better. The other dragons were friendly."

"They were," Sasha agreed. "I liked their human mates very much."

Max stole a quick kiss before tightening his grip on Sasha's hand and stepping forward. The air seemed thicker as it brushed against their bodies, but the pressure was only momentary. Their surroundings blurred before coming into focus again.

"What took you so long?" Blaze asked.

"I took a few moments to kiss my mate in private," Max said. He glanced at Noel and saw his brother was smiling and enjoying this adventure immensely.

"Let's go," Blaze said. "I'll introduce you to David and Rena. You can make arrangements, then we'd better fly home to see Mother and Father. Your disappearance upset them."

"All right," Sasha said, although she didn't sound happy, her expression telling him she worried regarding her parents' reaction to her human mate, and that did nothing to settle his anxiety.

Blaze led the way from the yew grove where they'd arrived. Beyond, an orchard stretched into the distance. Apple trees. Cherry trees. Orange and lemons. Peaches and pears.

In the distance, he could hear singing. Max soon spotted the male tenor. He wore a black robe and was busy weeding a vegetable plot. When he noticed them walking past, he lifted a hand in greeting.

"Do you know where David and Rena are at the moment?" Blaze called.

"They're in the communal room, trying to stop the older brothers from killing each other. They're voting on which part of the monastery business plan to concentrate on first," came the cheerful reply. "For once, I'm glad I'm a junior druid and need not bother myself over the decision making."

"What is this place?" Max asked.

"Remember I told you about the druids who power the barrier. This is the monastery where they live."

"Right, the reason I'm interviewing David and Rena."

Max wasn't sure what to expect since the dragons and his mate had decided it would be better for him to learn everything from David and Rena. The sound of raised voices traveled down a wide passage to the entrance. Blaze led them inside and stopped outside an open doorway. A dozen men wearing robes from red to blue and one gold gesticulated at each other and raised their voices to be better heard.

"Ah," Blaze said. "You wait here, and I'll wade into the crowd and let them know we've arrived." He plunged into the melee and tapped a man on the shoulder. He pivoted in their direction, and Max spotted a woman.

The young couple who walked toward them with welcoming smiles didn't fit what he'd conjured in his imagination. The woman wore jeans and a casual T-shirt, while the man dressed in the same manner as the male dragons in black trousers and a white linen shirt, open at the neck. He would've passed them on the street, apart from the fact they both sported an electric-blue tattoo on one side of their face. The whorls and interlaced knots of the tattoo were intricate and reminded him of Celtic scrollwork.

"Rena, David, this is my sister Sasha and her mate, Max. And this wee fellow is Noel. He's Max's younger brother."

"Your missing sister?" David asked, his gaze alert.

Blaze slipped his arm around Sasha's waist in affection. "She found herself and turned up at the cottage on Holy Island. Max is a reporter from the mainland, and Leo and the others decided it would be an excellent idea to produce a newspaper to let the Dragon Isles residents learn of all that has happened. They figured it would stop the spread of rumors and misinformation." Blaze shot a grin at Max. "If this works well, you might have a job here."

"That's a brilliant idea," Rena said. "We should've thought of that ourselves. You want to interview us and listen to our story? Have Liza, Leo, Cherry, and Martinos told you what happened to them?"

"I took plenty of notes," Max said. "Their stories are completed, and Leo, Liza, Martinos, and Cherry approved them for publication."

"I'll look after Noel while you and Sasha hear David's and Rena's story," Blaze said. "You noted Rena's weird hair?"

"Blaze! Did you leave your tact at the local pub?" Sasha snapped. "You do not say that sort of thing to a woman."

Rena grinned. "Your brother, Griffith, happened to my hair. He set it on fire while trying to burn his way out of a building here at the monastery."

Sasha's brows rose. "Griffith?"

"We won't let him forget this for quite a while," Blaze said with a chuckle.

David and Rena led them into a large room full of comfortable chairs and small tables.

"This is the solarium," David said. "The druids spend their evenings here relaxing after dinner. No one will interrupt us at this time of the day."

A druid hailed David and Rena, and the pair moved to speak with him.

"Would you like a tour?" Blaze asked Noel.

"Yes," Noel said, although Max didn't think his brother understood what a tour was. He placed his hand in Blaze's and ambled away without a backward glance.

"I've told you before, and no doubt, I'll tell you again, but you have worked magic with Noel," Max said, gazing after his brother.

He bore little resemblance to the clingy, whiny child he'd been after their parents' deaths. Understandable, of course, but with Sasha's help, Noel had gained confidence. He'd be forever grateful for the day she'd crashed through the barrier and into their lives.

Sasha shrugged. "I like Noel. He's a good kid."

"And I'm telling you, he has his moments. His behavior has improved with you around. Will your parents be all right with his differences? Your brothers haven't mentioned anything, but Noel's Down syndrome brings challenges. They'll become greater as he gets older."

"Our parents will treat him with kindness. I promise this. Noel is a child, and no matter what they say to us, they will not belittle Noel or act with nastiness toward him."

"Should I worry about our meeting with your parents?"

"No. Yes." Sasha shrugged. "I don't know. They were determined to betroth me to Bruceous."

"Sorry about that," Rena said with a smile. Apparently, her hair didn't bother her, and she glowed with happiness. "Things are still settling down after the upheaval we're going to tell you about, and some of the brothers require extra reassurance."

"Have a seat," David said. "We should be able to fit this in before lunch. Blaze mentioned you're flying to Perfume Isle to see your parents. I hope you'll eat with us before you leave."

"Thanks," Max said.

"Where should I start with my story?" David said.

"Start by telling Max and Sasha how you contacted me," Rena suggested.

"I'd prefer not to publicize this part," David said, his gaze on Max. "But it will help you to understand. I'm a dreamwalker. I inherited the ability from my mother, and using this skill, I contacted Rena." He continued with his tale, detailing the troubles at the monastery and how, through Rena, he'd joined forces with Leo and Martinos and their mates.

Max took notes, and even though he'd already learned part of the story, this seemed farfetched.

"It's all true," Rena said. "It took me a while to wrap my head around everything.

"Who is running the monastery now?" Max asked.

"Brother Colin is the head druid. He and a group of senior druids are slowly changing the way we used to do things." David paused. "Do you have everything you need to write your story?"

"I do," Max said. "Once I'm finished, I'll run the final version past you both. As I mentioned, Leo and Martinos have already approved their part of the story."

A bell tolled, and Rena rose. "Perfect timing. That's the lunch bell."

Lunch was a communal meal taken with the druids. They ate the hearty vegetable soup with fresh bread and cheese with a dessert of apple pie and custard.

"How long will you be on Perfume Isle?" Rena asked.

"One or two days," Sasha said. "It depends on how my parents react to my return with a human mate. This might be a fast trip."

"I'm sure you'll be fine," David said. "Your parents are reasonable, and they worried about your disappearance."

"I just hope they'll listen before they act," Sasha said with a wrinkle of her nose.

Once they'd finished lunch, they said their goodbyes and wandered outside to a cobblestone courtyard. Lemon trees planted in pots stood in a sunny corner while the perfume of a white flower drifted from a garden bed on their right.

"I'm still nervous about meeting your parents," Max confessed. "My lunch isn't sitting well. I've never had this trouble before."

"Us too," Sasha confessed. "But remember, we are mates, and Blaze and Griffith are on our side. We have options."

"Not really. Officially, I've absconded with Noel. The cops will be after me. My grandmother will insist on it. I have to make this work. Your parents have to like me."

"No, I mean we have options here. We can make our home base on Perfume Isle, or Martinos and Cherry offered us a place on Smoking Isle. Our decision need not come right away. We have the luxury of time to make our choice. Maybe once your friend discovers what's going on with your grandmother, we can return to Bamburgh. I'm sure we can help the dragons on Dragon Isle and earn a living too."

"God," Max said, relief pulsing through him at her reasonable tone and suggestions. "My past girlfriends would've had a tantrum by now. You're so calm and logical."

"Not always," Sasha said, her tone dry. "Ask my family."

Max grasped her hand and gave it a quick squeeze. "I can't see it myself, but I'll take your word for it."

"Are you ready to go?" Blaze asked.

"No," Max said.

Griffith laughed. "I don't know what Sasha told you, but our parents are reasonable dragons. They won't burn you at first sight. Second maybe." His eyes twinkled with mirth, and Sasha slapped him on the arm.

"Knock it off. I know they can't stop us being together because we're mates, but their support means something to me. Would you rather have Bruceous as part of the family?" Sasha asked, her tone tart.

Noel tugged on Max's shirt. "Can I ride with Blaze?"

"Not today, buddy. You need to grow bigger and stronger before you can ride on your own."

"How?" Noel's voice came close to a moan.

"You know those vegetables you refused to eat last night," Sasha said.

"Yes." Noel stared at Max and Sasha as he waited for an explanation.

"Eating your vegetables is the best way to stay strong," she shared.

Griffith let out a guffaw, and Blaze joined in the hilarity.

"Stop laughing," Sasha muttered. "A healthy diet is important to grow. Liza told Joanna the same thing last night."

"Do you know who you sound like?" Blaze asked.

Griffith continued to chortle and shake his head.

Sasha groaned. "I sound like a parent. That's because I am a parent. Max and I need to make sure Noel grows up with values and is hale and hearty. Laugh all you want, but I care for Max and for Noel. That means I act like a mature dragon."

"I love you," Max said, the words bursting from him.

Sasha grinned and threw herself at him. He kissed her, despite their audience. Like everything, Sasha gave the kiss her all, and they were both breathing hard when their lips parted.

"I wanna see," Noel protested and peeled Griffith's hands away from his eyes.

Blaze pulled a face. "Let's fly, otherwise it will be late by the time we arrive. I wanted to give Max a tour of the estate and maybe take him to House of Ghan to meet Rafael."

"Your other brother?" Max asked.

"Yes." Sasha stepped away from him and started stripping while her brothers did the same.

Max crouched in front of Noel and fastened his jacket. He placed a warm hat on his brother's head and wound a scarf around his neck. Max donned warm clothes too before scooping up the discarded ones and packing them in a fabric bag.

Soon, they were flying across the monastery land and over the sea beyond. The flight went way too fast for Max's liking, and even though he was certain of Sasha, he stressed about her parents' reaction to her mating with a human. Blaze and Griffith seemed to have accepted him already, but that didn't stop trepidation from marching through Max and slapping around his confidence.

"How are you and Noel doing?" Sasha asked through their private channel.

"We're good. It's cold, but flying has Noel enthralled. He won't want to travel any other way."

Sasha and her dragon both laughed as he meant them to, and the gaiety eased some of his tension. An hour later, he spotted land. *"Is that Perfume Isle?"*

"It is," Sasha said. *"You should smell sweet spices soon. Our island is famous for its delectable scent."*

Sasha's dragon flapped her wings and arrowed downward until

she skimmed the treetops. Sasha was right. The perfume from the plants reminded him of his mother's cookies when they'd come fresh from the oven. A pang struck his chest as he thought of his mother and, by extension, his father. He missed them, even though he hadn't spent much time in Bamburgh. He'd still made regular calls via the internet or phone. They would've loved Sasha. His parents hadn't liked his fiancée much. They'd been polite with her, but he'd sensed their reservations, and once he'd overheard them discussing the engagement. He doubted they'd have the same issues with Sasha, despite her otherness.

He prayed Sasha's parents were open-minded enough to give him a chance.

"Our home is over that hill," Sasha said.

Although Max had expected a prosperous estate—given what Sasha, Blaze, and Griffith had told him about their home—this was even grander than he'd anticipated. The buildings were of weathered gray stone, and like the monastery, the gardens were a show of flowers and herbs. Beyond, large orchards of fragrant trees emitted the sweet aroma of baking spices. Max wasn't sure what the trees were, but they contributed to the wealth of the Mountholden dragon clan.

They landed in a large grassy area in front of the stone mansion. Max clambered down from Sasha's back and reached up to help his brother. He tugged Noel out of the way, giving the three siblings plenty of space to shift to their human forms.

"Did you enjoy the flight, Noel?" Max asked.

"Yes." Noel's eyes shone with enthusiasm. "I'm going to draw pictures to show Joanna. She's my friend."

"You do that," Max said.

Sasha dressed rapidly, as did Blaze and Griffith.

A woman appeared from the direction of the flower gardens. She was running and shouting at the same time. "Tiberius! Tiberius! Come quickly."

A man strode from a smaller building nearby, his hair a light brown with strands of copper. One look at the man's broad shoulders and height told Max this was Sasha's father. The dragon scanned the new arrivals, and when his gaze settled on Sasha, he lengthened his strides to hurry to his daughter.

"You found her," Sasha's mother cried, and she kept running until she reached Sasha. She wrapped her arms around her daughter and clung to her. Tiberius hustled to his wife and daughter and drew them both into his embrace.

"This might take a while," Griffith said as he fastened the ties on the front of his shirt.

Blaze came over to join them and stood watching his parents and sister with a grin on his face.

"Who are they?" Noel asked in a loud voice.

"That's our mother and father," Blaze said.

"I don't have a mother and father," Noel said.

Max winced. "That's not true, buddy. Remember, they've gone

to heaven. We'll see them again one day."

Blaze slapped Max on the shoulder in silent sympathy. "Noel, you can share my parents if you want."

Max sent Blaze a grateful glance.

"Mother, please. You're smothering me," Sasha protested after a long time. "Please, I need to breathe."

Tiberius laughed. "Dalinda, let Sasha go so she can tell us where she has been all this time."

"Excellent idea, husband." Dalinda released her grip on Sasha and stood back. She slid against her husband's side and glared at Sasha. "You worried us silly, child. You vanished without warning, and none of us could find you. Blaze, Griffith, and even Rafael have searched the Dragon Isles for you."

Sasha crossed to Max and extended her hand. Silently, Max clasped their fingers, and together, they turned to face Tiberius and Dalinda Mountholden. "This is Max Lombardy, my mate, and his younger brother Noel."

For a moment, silence fell, then both of Sasha's parents lifted their heads. Their nostrils flared in the same manner Max had noticed the other dragons use when they were attempting to identify something or someone.

Tiberius frowned. "They're human, but they hold your scent."

"Because Max is my mate," Sasha repeated.

"You've been hiding in the human village," Dalinda said in clear disapproval.

"Mother, please listen to Sasha instead of jumping to conclusions," Blaze said.

Max sent him another grateful smile.

"We've traveled from the monastery on Smoking Isle," Griffith said. "I'm starving. Can we have something to eat and drink while we discuss where Sasha has been and why it has taken her so long to return home?"

"Good idea," Blaze said and shunted their mother toward a door over to their right.

Noel marched over to Tiberius and tugged on his hand. Surprised, Tiberius glanced down at the boy. "Are you a dragon?" Noel asked.

"Yes," Tiberius said.

Noel held out his hand for Tiberius to take. "I like dragons. Shasha is a dragon."

Tiberius led Noel over to Dalinda, and Noel held out his free hand to Sasha's mother. Dalinda laughed, the sound a delighted tinkle.

"Your brother has cut through their bluster," Blaze said in a low voice. "You're lucky to have him along."

Sasha grinned at the interaction between her parents and Noel. Max groaned when his brother asked if they had cookies because he loved the ones Sasha made him.

"Don't worry," Sasha whispered with a tearful smile. "Everything is going to be fine."

Max thought so too, but there was always an outside chance they might keep his brother and kick Max out for daring to touch their daughter. Sasha urged him to follow her parents and brothers, and Max walked at her side.

Sasha led him into a large room that turned out to be a kitchen. Two women wearing white aprons to protect their gowns were busy toiling at a sturdy wooden table. One was peeling what looked like a root vegetable while the other was stirring the contents of a large bowl.

"Normally, we'd sit in here, but for this conversation, I believe we'll go into the formal dining room," Dalinda said. "Sasha, show Max and his brother to the dining room while I organize tea." She turned to Max. "What will Noel drink?"

"Noel likes milk," Sasha said. "Come on, Max. This way."

Max was aware of Tiberius following closely behind while Blaze and Griffith remained behind to chat with their mother.

The dining room held bulky wooden chairs and a sturdy table that looked as if it would comfortably seat a dozen people. Decorative cushions sat on each chair.

"Sit here," Sasha said in a quiet voice. She tugged out another chair for Noel and helped him to clamber up while Max took stock of the rest of the room. The space was as clean as the kitchen had been, and the wooden surfaces gleamed from frequent polishing. A floral scent drifted through an open window. A large painting of the ocean on a stormy day dominated one wall of the room.

Tiberius took a seat at the head of the table while Sasha sat beside Max. Blaze and Griffith entered, banter racing between them. Blaze sat on the other side of Noel.

Dalinda bustled into the room, not long afterward. "Our meal won't be long." She sat at the other end of the table, making it clear as to their position of authority within the family. "Right, young lady. Where have you been?"

"I flew over the sea before going to visit my friend. Anger drove me after our conversation about Bruceous. I thought to fly off some of my temper."

Tiberius and Dalinda exchanged a glance before turning their attention back to Sasha.

"Go on," Tiberius said.

"While I was flying, the air turned thick, and it was like fighting through heavy syrup. I kept flying, and the next minute, I spotted a long sandy beach. I wasn't sure of my location and landed to get my bearings. It turned out I'd crossed through the barrier and ended up on the mainland. My dragon and I heard crying, and we shifted and dressed before investigating. I found Noel. He'd become lost. I helped him and met Max, who offered me a job looking after Noel. Since I already liked Noel, and it was apparent Max cared for his brother, plus I needed somewhere to stay, I accepted. The more I got to know Max and Noel, the more I liked them.

"When Max's grandmother paid people to kidnap Noel, I had to shift to my dragon form to save him. Things became worse when

Max's grandmother involved the law, and they ordered Max to give Noel to her. We journeyed to Holy Island to avoid the reporters, the grandmother, and the law. By this time, Max knew I was a dragon, and he said we should check the barrier in case I could travel home. The barrier was strong and impassable, but we met Liza and Cherry on the beach. I smelled the dragon on them, and we followed their trail. That's where we met Blaze."

Tiberius glanced from Sasha to Max and back. "You left out the part where you became mates."

"I—" Sasha began.

"Let me answer this one," Max said. "Your daughter is amazing. She's unlike any other woman I've met. She's smart and beautiful."

"You forgot gorgeous," Sasha's dragon shrieked.

Max smiled and winked at Sasha. "She's gorgeous. Adaptable. Sensible. She loves Noel and taught him to swim. It's been amazing watching my brother bloom under her care. Our parents died in an accident just over six months ago, and it has been difficult. I had to work, and my grandmother was toiling behind the scenes to take Noel from me."

Tiberius frowned. "He's not normal."

"Don't say that," Sasha snapped, acting the mama bear without hesitation. "There is nothing wrong with Noel."

Everyone stared at Sasha in surprise, everyone apart from Max. He'd learned how protective Sasha was of people she loved.

"My brother was born with a condition called Down syndrome.

257

It means he has an extra chromosome."

"Which makes him special," Sasha snapped, glaring at each of her family members.

"What's a chromosome?" Blaze asked.

"It's part of every living thing and holds our genetic code," Max said.

When everyone looked blank, Sasha said, "We need a Justine, The Smart Computer, here to help everyone learn mainland stuff." She wrinkled her nose. "Everything is more advanced on the mainland. Humans are smart and have progressed faster than our people."

"Then the outlandish stories Blaze and Griffith have been telling me are true?" Tiberius asked.

"Yes," Sasha said, clenching her hands beneath the table. "I will say this only once. I refuse to become the wife of Bruceous. He spends his time pinching bottoms at social gatherings but does it on the sly. I have my suspicions he forces some dragon women into having sex with him. For you to compel me to marry him is ludicrous."

"Sasha will marry me," Max said. "Or at least, I intend to ask her once the moment is right."

"Mother. Father. We are already mates. Everyone believed the old tales of mates were pure fiction, but Leo, Martinos, and I have discovered our true mates. Each of us has a human mate. It is wrong for you to consider even trying to part us. It would be cruel.

Wait, why are you smiling?" Her eyes narrowed as she stared at her parents.

"We never intended for you to become Bruceous's wife," Dalinda said. "But it concerned us when you turned down every eligible offer."

"Child, we could sense your restlessness," Tiberius said. "You needed an adventure of sorts." His brows drew together. "We didn't envision you bursting through the barrier and taking on the mainland, but it appears we underestimated you. You have not only had your adventure, but you have thrived."

"Wait, you were intent on pushing me to act on my own?" Sasha asked, her confusion clear.

"We didn't want you to follow in the footsteps of your friend and agree to marry a much older dragon to have your own home," her mother said.

"We didn't expect you to disappear without warning or to bring back a human mate." Tiberius glanced at Noel and grinned. "Or a child."

"What are your plans now? Will you stay on Perfume Isle?" Dalinda asked.

"Family is important to Sasha," Max said before Sasha could speak. "We'd like to have a base here, but we will also spend time on the other islands with Leo and Liza, and Martinos and Cherry, plus David and Rena. It doesn't feel right to abscond with Noel and have the law on our tail. I'd like to clear my name on the mainland, which means traveling back there sometimes."

"I'm going with you to the mainland," Blaze said.

"Me too," Griffith said at the same time.

"We can arrange that if everyone agrees, the visit is a good idea," Max said.

"Cherry and Martinos are moving to Bamburgh," Blaze said. "We have a plan to work together and slowly introduce a few chosen dragons."

"We can't have dragons flying everywhere," Max said.

"The newspapermen saw me," Sasha said, "although they didn't know it was me. Any dragons who travel to the mainland must keep to their human forms unless it's a matter of life or death."

"We've already agreed to those terms with the others," Griffith said.

"We understand the dangers to us as a species. Sasha, we told you what happened here while you were on the mainland." Blaze glanced at his parents. "You haven't heard everything. Max is a reporter. He is writing the stories to go into a newspaper."

When Tiberius and Dalinda exchanged a puzzled glance, Max wondered if the dragons and humans here could read. He'd thought Sasha had told him they could. Before he could ask questions, Sasha enlightened him.

"If we wish to impart news here on Perfume Isle, we pin posters up in several strategic places. The other islands do the same. A newspaper will be radical for the Dragon Isles' residents. A step toward progress. It's an excellent idea," Sasha said. "I wish we could have the internet here along with Justine, The Smart Computer. I liked Justine very much, and she taught me a lot."

"Communication is important," Tiberius conceded.

Max nodded, surprised a little by the calm acceptance of something unfamiliar.

"My love," Tiberius said, grinning at his wife.

Max stilled at the salacious expression on the dragon's face. He glanced at Dalinda and discovered an answering smirk on her face.

"Your plan worked," Tiberius said. "Sasha has a mate, Blaze and Griffith wish to spread their wings and explore the mainland, while Rafael remains at the House of Ghan. We will have our home to ourselves." He waggled his brows.

"Eew," Sasha's dragon screeched. *"They're talking about kissing and sex."*

"We kiss," Max pointed out along their private communication path.

"We're young. They're old," Sasha's dragon snapped.

Max glanced at Tiberius and Dalinda again and grinned. "I'm so glad I met Sasha. She has changed my life."

"You treat our daughter well, and we won't have any problems," Tiberius said.

"And don't turn up without giving us a warning," Dalinda chirped and waggled her eyebrows, aping her husband. "We might be busy."

Max bit his lip to halt his laughter as Blaze's mouth dropped open. Clear shock etched into Griffith's features while Sasha wrinkled her nose.

"We should not be having this conversation in front of Noel," Sasha said.

"I like kissing," Noel said, and he leaned closer to Blaze and made a loud kissing sound against Blaze's cheek.

Max chuckled along with the others. His chest felt tight and full, and he realized this was happiness. Sasha had charged into his life and changed everything for the better. She'd filled the aching hole inside him after he'd lost his parents and become responsible for his brother. While he still mourned their loss, he'd released his panic and the out-of-control sensation that had buried him with worry and stress. He reached under the table and placed his hand on Sasha's knee, squeezing lightly. "I love you, Sasha."

She smiled at him, everything she felt on her face. "I love you, too."

And she leaned over to kiss him on the lips. It was a firm kiss that had him longing for more. Privacy, for one.

"Max and Sasha like kissing too," Noel said. "They kiss lots."

"It means they're happy and like each other," Blaze said. "Would you like to see my orchard? It's full of beautiful trees."

"Are there butterflies?" Noel asked.

"I think so," Griffith said. "I'll help you look for butterflies.

Tiberius stood. "Dalinda and I are off to celebrate our new

freedom."

"*Eew!*" Sasha's dragon shouted. "*I don't want to hear that stuff.*"

Max laughed. "*Why don't you give me a tour of the place? Show me your bedroom.*"

Sasha jumped to her feet. "*That is an excellent idea. We'll make my private wing the last halt on our tour.*"

Max took her hand in his and wandered where she led, taking in the comfortable and sometimes expensive furnishings. It was obvious Sasha's family was wealthy by any standards. There were the family rooms where they relaxed and more formal rooms to host guests and a solarium.

Everything was spotlessly clean without a thing out of place. This house didn't say *lived in*—not like his parents' property at Bamburgh—but it was still a spectacular residence.

"Did you want to live here or find our own place on one of the islands?" Max asked.

"I want a smaller place," Sasha confided. "Somewhere where we are comfortable and can relax."

"Sounds perfect to me."

"We don't need to make a quick decision," Sasha said. "We have time." She stopped outside a thick wooden door with carved panels. "This is my chamber."

She opened the door and led Max inside. Max scanned the enormous bed, currently streamed with sunshine, before shutting the door behind them. A sharp clunk sounded as he shot the sturdy lock to bar surprise visitors.

"I'm so glad you're here with me," Sasha said.

"I wouldn't be anywhere else," Max said and took her into his arms. An instant later, their lips met. Max took his time kissing Sasha, enjoying the hell out of the intimacy. They were both breathing hard when the kiss ended. Max pressed his forehead to Sasha's and breathed in her scent. "I'm feeling tired. What do you say to a rest before we rejoin your family?"

"*Yay!*" her dragon cried.

Max chuckled, and Sasha watched the happiness in his features, the sparkle in his blue eyes, and the sensual intent. An answering heat roared through her.

"I think a rest is a perfect idea. Blaze and Griffith will watch Noel. You can trust them with his safety."

"I know," Max said, prowling across the space between them. "Your brothers have been great with Noel, but I don't wish to discuss brothers right now."

"*Hee-haw!*" her dragon shouted.

"Shush," Max whispered, and he kissed her again, his touch igniting desire and lust and yearning. His hands glided across her shoulders and down her back. Sasha relaxed against his broad chest and savored the heat igniting between them. He licked the seam of her mouth, urging her to open for him.

She moaned, his questing fingers shaping and massaging her

breast through her clothes. The barrier eventually became too much, and she wriggled away and ripped off the T-shirt she was wearing. She stepped closer to Max and unfastened his shirt buttons one by one. Each bit of flesh revealed enticed her to plant a kiss on his torso. She loved his scent and the warmth of his skin, the swift intake of air he took each time her lips grazed his body.

Soon their clothes melted away, left in a trail as they made their way across the room. Max lifted her and placed her on the bed. In the next instant, he was beside her and kissing her again. Hands wandered and explored, and Sasha enjoyed herself immensely. She kissed Max's neck, his flat nipples, teasing groans and sighs from her man. Gradually, she moved down his body, fascinated by their differences.

"Reading a kissing book and doing the exploring myself is quite different," she whispered.

"I should hope so." Max's grin took the sting from his words. "What will you do when your Kindle runs out of charge, or you read the last of your kissing books?"

"We must visit Cherry at her bookstore. I think we visited the one Cherry and Martinos intend to purchase." Sasha curled her fingers around his cock and lightly squeezed. "You feel hot."

"That's what you do to me," Max said, the lazy gleam in his eyes enticing her to continue.

She gripped his shaft and pumped up and down, fascinated by the bead of liquid that formed on his tip. Curious, she bent her head and licked away the droplet.

"God, Sasha."

Encouraged, she took more of him into her mouth and explored with her lips and tongue. Max's fingers curled into her hair, the faint sting bringing a reaction in her too.

"Take me deeper," Max said. "Place your hands at the base of my shaft so you can control how much goes into your mouth."

"This feels good?"

"Do you enjoy it when I lick your sex?"

"Yes."

"There's your answer, then. If your mouth on me felt any better, I might expire. Now lick me and suck. Once I get closer to my orgasm, I'll want to thrust. Don't let me overwhelm you."

Sasha followed Max's instructions and took pleasure from his groans and the way he fisted her hair. The sting of pain each time his fingers tightened produced a pulse of enjoyment in her sex.

"Enough," Max said, pulling away.

"You want to stop?"

He grinned at her. "Hell no. I want to come inside you." He lifted her away and placed her beneath him, covering her body and making her feel feminine. Using his knee, he nudged her thighs apart, lined up his cock, and pushed inside her.

The sense of fullness pleased her too, and she gripped his shoulders, lifting into each of his strokes. "Yes," she hissed.

He nibbled her neck and ran his fingers over her dragon tattoo, doubling the delightful sensations running through her. Without warning, Max pulled free. Before she could protest that he'd ruined everything, he lifted her and guided her onto her hands and knees. He covered her from behind, and the new position delighted her.

"Touch yourself," he whispered against her ear.

She did as he suggested while he pinched and tweaked her nipples. Sasha closed her eyes, excited by the contact with Max. The strokes. The caresses. The lazy glide of her fingers against her clit. Each sensation swelled, growing and growing until she could bear them no longer. She shattered, her channel squeezing around Max's cock in quick spasms. Max groaned against her ear, and he pinched one of her nipples again. The streak of pain set off another series of delightful twitches, and she gasped in unison with Max. His hips jerked in several rapid thrusts before he stilled, and she could feel and hear his pleasure as he came.

"You are amazing," Max whispered, long moments later when they both reclined, and Max had his arms wrapped around her.

"Right back at you. I'm so glad we met you. I don't truly believe my parents when they said they were joking about Bruceous. My mother was convincing when she told me about the pending betrothal."

"I have to meet this Bruceous character."

"No doubt you will," Sasha said. "My father and brothers do business with him, so he attends many of our gatherings."

"Don't worry. You're safe. You're my mate, and according to Leo and Martinos, no one would ever try to separate a mated couple."

"That's true," Sasha said, feeling more cheerful at the reminder. "Besides, I love you."

"I like this kissing business," her dragon said with a throaty groan.

"So now, you're awake," Max teased. "This is very weird, you know. It's like having two women in my bed. Have you read kissing books where there are more than two lovers?"

"No," Sasha said, not having to force her intrigue. "Two how?"

"One woman and two men or one man and two women," Max said. "Sometimes more and in different combinations."

"We have to read some of those kissing books," her dragon declared.

"As long as you realize, it's only ever going to be us," Max said with laughter in his voice. "I will never welcome more men or women into our bed. Wait, maybe we should read those kissing books together. How does that sound?"

"Yes," Sasha said and kissed Max on his shoulder.

"Yes," her dragon echoed and did a wee boogie over Sasha's shoulder and onto her back.

"I love you, Sasha. All of you, and I'm going to spend the rest of my life, proving that to you."

"I told you we were gorgeous," her dragon piped up.

Sasha chuckled. "You did." She turned serious. "I love you too."

"We're perfect for one another," her dragon announced.

Max grinned. "There was never any doubt about that. I thought it the moment I spotted you."

"*Aw,*" her dragon said and yawned. *"I'm tired now. I'm going to sleep.*"

Sasha rolled her eyes and cuddled closer to Max. "We don't have to sleep."

Max's eyes darkened, and he drew her closer. They didn't have a rest for a long, long time.

EPILOGUE

M ax's phone rang, and he glanced at it in surprise. They'd been staying on Holy Island while they printed the newspaper he'd written—more of a newsletter really—using a desktop publishing program. Sasha was collating the papers for him while he kept the printer stocked with paper and ink.

Sasha paused with her stapling. "Who is it?"

"Jerome. My private investigator friend."

"Answer it. He might have news. It would be wonderful if you didn't have to hide Noel and could visit the mainland whenever you wanted."

The phone stopped ringing before it restarted. It was his friend again. "Jerome," Max greeted his caller.

"I've got the proof for you. I've already mentioned your grandmother has a gambling problem and mortgaged the house without telling your grandfather. She thought she'd regain her losses, but things didn't work out for her. She borrowed money from a local biker gang, and they want their money plus interest back. When I couldn't get hold of you, I contacted my friend on the police force and told him everything. I also gave him copies of the evidence I'd found. It's obvious that since the bank has foreclosed on the mortgage, they no longer have a home. Your grandfather didn't know a lot of this, and he walked out on your grandmother. He told me he's sorry, and it was never his intention to cut you from Noel's life. He wants to see you and Noel and maintain a familial relationship."

"How did he not understand what was going on?" Max demanded. "He must've known of the legal matters my grandmother instigated."

"Your grandfather said he had other business interests he was taking care of, and he'd had to take a business trip to Paris. He'd been away for a week, which was when everything unraveled for your grandmother."

"What happens next?" Sasha stood by him and placed her hand on his shoulder in silent commiseration.

Jerome must've caught her question because he said, "The cops have dropped the charges, but I believe the Family Court judge wants to see you and Noel. I think the judge wants to reassure himself of Noel's safety and happiness."

"What do I need to do?"

"I checked your mailbox. There is mail there that looks as if it's from the court."

"Open it," Max said decisively.

Paper rustled, and a few minutes later, Jerome spoke. "They've made an appointment for next week. A social worker will interview you at your house. She wants to see you and Noel together and separately. Once she completes her report, the judge will see you the following week."

"That's quick," Max muttered.

"It says here that since a young child is part of this mess, they want it sorted as soon as possible or words to that effect."

"I see," Max said. "Are you certain I won't get arrested once I arrive at home?"

"The police became concerned when you didn't show up with Noel as ordered, but once I gave them the evidence I'd collected, they understood. The judge may reprimand you, but I doubt they'll remove Noel from your custody."

"But there is always that possibility," Max said in a dark voice. "My grandmother manipulated me into taking that job in Edinburgh. How do I know the judge isn't in her pocket?"

"Didn't I mention the police arrested your grandmother?" Jerome said. "She's in jail, and they refused to give her bail."

"Hell," Max said, startled by the revelation. "All right. I'll think about this. Email your bill, and I'll pay you straight away. I owe you more than I can say. Noel is happy with me. My grandmother made him stressed."

"Because kids can sense when adults are going through the motions," Jerome said.

"Thanks," Max said.

"Catch ya later." An instant later, Jerome disconnected the call.

"What are you going to do?" Sasha asked.

"Jerome is right. I have to take the risk this will turn out all right, and the judge will award me full custody. If something goes wrong, we can always disappear again. You are our secret weapon."

"Ooh," her dragon said, entering the conversation for the first time. *"I'm going to be a spy lady."*

"Only if we need to. It's the last resort," Sasha said.

"We'd better retrieve Noel from Leo and Liza and ask if we can borrow a car to get to the mainland. It's best if we don't fly this time."

"Agreed," Sasha said.

Three days later, they were back at Max's house, close to the town of Bamburgh.

"What does one wear to meet a social worker?" Sasha asked.

Max smiled, but it appeared forced. This social worker wielded power with the court and the judge. They had to make a favorable impression. "Wear something smart. A skirt and a nice blouse."

"We have the right clothes," Sasha's dragon informed him. *"Don't*

worry. If the social worker is horrid, we'll throw flames at them."

Max groaned.

"That was easy," Sasha said with a chuckle. "We're teasing. We will be on our best behavior. I've made cookies and will make tea. Noel is busy drawing pictures."

"What if Noel tells her about the Dragon Isles?" Max asked.

"If he does, we'll spin it and tell her it's a story we've invented. Don't worry. Get ready."

They were back in the kitchen when the doorbell buzzed.

"I'll get it," Sasha said, her face softening at his grimace. "We've got this."

All Max could think of was the number of things that might go wrong.

Sasha's voice carried back to him as she greeted the social worker. "This is Karen," she said as she ushered the middle-aged woman back into the room. "This is Max, my fiancée, and this is Noel."

"Hello," Karen said.

She was an older woman with lines of experience bracketing her mouth and radiating from the corners of her blue eyes. She wore a teal cotton skirt with a plain white blouse and what his mother had called, with a wrinkle of her nose, sensible shoes.

"Have a seat," Max said, gesturing at the kitchen table, which thanks to Sasha, was impeccably clean. "We were about to have a morning tea break. Tea?"

"That sounds lovely. Milk, no sugar, please." Karen smiled and took the chair Max had indicated. She set her briefcase beside her. "Do I smell chocolate chip biscuits?"

"You do," Sasha said. "They're Noel's favorite, so he helped me make a batch this morning." She grinned at Noel, who was sitting at the table and drawing in his book. He'd tucked his tongue between his teeth as he so often did while concentrating.

"Hello, Noel," Karen said. "My name is Karen. I enjoy drawing plants and flowers. What are you drawing today?"

Noel glanced up at her, and Max gave a silent prayer his brother would talk to the woman. Sometimes, he was quiet with strangers and didn't present well.

"Dragons," Noel said. "I like dragons."

"They are magnificent creatures," Karen agreed.

"Has she met a dragon?" Sasha's dragon demanded through their private channel.

"No, she means the ones on television," Max replied, automatically thinking his response. *"She's probably attempting to empathize with Noel and find common ground."*

"Oh," Sasha's dragon said in a dismissive tone. *"The dragons on TV are silly. They're not gorgeous like us."*

"Nor do they have such an inflated opinion of themselves," Sasha said drily.

"But, we are gorgeous."

"Yes, you are," Max said firmly. *"Now, shush. We need to pay attention to Karen."*

"What else do you like to do?" Karen asked Noel.

Max made himself help Sasha and handed Karen her tea while he silently prompted Noel to respond.

His brother hesitated before glancing at Sasha. "I help Shasha do jobs and grow plants in the garden. Swimming. Shasha is teaching me. Max reads me stories, and we visit the castle."

"Bamburgh Castle?"

Noel bobbed his head.

"What else?" Karen asked. "Do you go to kindy?"

"Yes," Noel said.

"Milk and cookies?" Sasha asked Noel.

"Yes, please," Noel said.

Pride swelled in Max. Noel was handling this meeting well.

"We'll pop your coloring aside for later, buddy, so you don't get crumbs on your dragons." Max packed up the coloring pencils and Noel's book and set them aside.

"What do you do to stimulate Noel and help him learn?" Karen asked.

"Both Sasha and I teach him small tasks and repeat them until he learns them. He loves the beach, and either Sasha or I take him walking or swimming most days. He enjoys getting outside and likes nature. His strength and coordination have improved a lot in the last few months."

"He's looking healthy and happy. Even in this short time, I can see he's comfortable with you and your fiancée. Have you set a date yet for your marriage?"

"Not yet, but it will be soon," Max said with a wink at Sasha. "Our engagement celebration took a back seat after my parents' accident. I'll admit striking a proper home-work balance has been difficult, but Sasha has helped. She stepped in when my mother's previous helper started drinking on the job."

"Your grandmother stated you fired the woman for no reason." Karen rifled through a file. "Yes, that is what she said in her statement." Karen jotted a note, then lifted her head to peer at both him and Sasha.

"I found Noel wandering around outside when I arrived home," Sasha said. "Max came not long afterward, and we discovered Sheryl passed out in her room. There was an almost empty bottle of alcohol on her side table."

"She was drunk," Max said firmly. "The fumes almost knocked me over once she woke and spoke to me. I told her to leave immediately, and Sasha offered to step into the void."

Karen sipped her tea and set down her empty mug. "What about a job? I understand you are unemployed at present."

"I intend to do freelance journalism, and in between stories, I've agreed to help a friend in his art gallery in Bamburgh. He and his wife have purchased the old bookstore there and one of the adjoining buildings, they've turned into a gallery to showcase my friend's work plus that of local artists."

"And that would mean you'd be at home with Noel most

nights?" Karen asked.

"Yes, that was partly the reason I accepted the job. Plus, it's a challenge. I want to help my friend do well."

Karen picked up her handbag. "Would you mind showing me Noel's bedroom?"

Max stood. "Yes, this way, please." He guided her through the house and up the stairs to the second level. At the end of the landing, he pushed open Noel's bedroom door and stepped aside. One wall was an art gallery of Noel's paintings and drawings while a framed photo of their parents sat beside Noel's bed. His toy box was open, and a teddy bear sat propped against his pillow.

"Does he dress himself?"

"Yes. He prefers to dress himself. Sasha and I guide him in clothes choice and make sure he showers and keeps clean. He likes to learn how to do things for himself and perseveres until he conquers a task. It's not always easy, and he gets frustrated, but he's doing well."

Karen nodded. "I have everything I need to complete my report. We will contact you in the next few days."

"I thought you'd spend longer with us," Max said.

"Normally, it would take longer, but because of the circumstances, we are pushing Noel's case through the system. It's imperative a child is settled and happy. Given his Down syndrome, we don't want to jeopardize Noel's advancement. You will hear from us by the end of the week." She smiled and patted Max's arm briefly when he scowled. "Don't worry. I am thrilled with everything I've seen here today."

Karen left, and Max and Sasha exchanged a glance.

"I need to keep busy," Max said. "Otherwise, I'll go crazy. What do you say to driving to Bamburgh and helping Cherry and Martinos with their cleaning? Noel can take his coloring, and we can go for ice cream or a walk in the park."

"Done deal," Sasha said.

An hour later, they were in Bamburgh, working alongside Martinos, Cherry, Liza, and Rena. Max's phone rang, and he took it from his pocket to check the number calling.

"My lawyer," Max said, his stomach flipping.

"Answer it," Sasha said.

Everyone else fell silent as Max spoke. "Hello."

"Good news for you, Max. Your grandmother has stopped proceedings against you. The social worker wrote a complimentary report about Noel's progress, and her report went to the judge along with a copy for us and your grandmother's lawyer. The judge dismissed the case, and you're officially Noel's legal guardian."

Sasha beamed at him while Martinos whispered details of the call to Liza and Rena.

"What will happen to my grandmother?"

"She is facing charges of attempted kidnapping along with others relating to fraudulent claims, which brings me to your grandfather. He insists he knew nothing of his wife's schemes. He wants to continue visiting you both with prior notice, of course. What do you want me to tell him?"

"He is welcome to visit Noel and me," Max said. "Tell him to ring first, though, since Sasha and I intend to travel a bit and take Noel with us."

"Will do," his lawyer said. "I'll send you details in writing, but congratulations. You've won."

"Thank you," Max said. "We appreciate your help."

The lawyer chuckled. "I'll send my bill. Any questions?"

"No," Max said. "Thanks." He hung up, and Sasha threw her arms around his neck and hugged him.

"It's over," she said.

"It is," he agreed.

"We can organize a wedding now," Cherry said.

"We can," Max said. "Anything Sasha wants."

Which was how the minister at the human village on Hissing Isle stood before them a week later. Both humans and dragons packed the church, their high spirits resounding through the interior. The late afternoon sun glinted through the rose window above them. Max held Sasha's hands in his and repeated his vows.

Sasha grinned at him, her dragon reflected in her eyes as she accepted him as her husband.

"You may now kiss the bride," Allen said, his eyes twinkling as several cheers rang out in the church interior.

Max took Sasha in his arms and kissed her gently before

deepening the contact. Shouts and applause filled the church—a few wolf-whistles. Max pulled away from Sasha, and as one, they turned to face their friends and family.

"I love you, Sasha," Max murmured.

"I know," Sasha said. "Right back at you."

"Of course you love us," Sasha's dragon retorted as they walked down the aisle. *"We're gorgeous."*

And that was the truth, Max thought as they received congratulations. He was a lucky man, since he'd enjoyed the entire journey with Sasha. Their future lay before them, and Max couldn't wait to experience the rest of the adventure with his wife and mate at his side.

Want More Sasha?

Not quite ready to let Max and Sasha go? Me neither. Learn what happens when Sasha rescues Max's grandfather in this bonus short story! You'll also receive a copy of the cover that inspired the entire Dragon Isles series.

Visit here (https://dl.bookfunnel.com/z9xk8viykf) for your free bonus story.

About Shelley

USA Today bestselling author Shelley Munro lives in Auckland, the City of Sails, with her husband and a cheeky Jack Russell/mystery breed dog.

Typical New Zealanders, Shelley and her husband left home for their big OE soon after they married (translation of New Zealand speak - big overseas experience). A twelve-month-long adventure lengthened to six years of roaming the world. Enduring memories include being almost sat on by a mountain gorilla in Rwanda, lazing on white sandy beaches in India, whale watching in Alaska, searching for leprechauns in Ireland, and dealing with ghosts in an English pub.

While travel is still a big attraction, these days Shelley is most likely found in front of her computer following another love - that of writing stories of contemporary and paranormal romance and adventure. Other interests include watching rugby (strictly for research purposes), cycling, playing croquet and the ukelele, and curling up with an enjoyable book.

Visit Shelley at her Website

https://shelleymunro.com

Join Shelley's Newsletter

https://shelleymunro.com/newsletter

Also By Shelley

My Precious Gift

My Grumpy Wolf

Middlemarch Gathering

My Highland Mate

My Highland Fling

My Elusive Mate

My Valiant Princess

My Highland Wedding

My Highland Billionaire

Dragon Investigators

Blue Moon Dragon

Blood Moon Dragon

Black Moon Dragon

Snow Moon Dragon

Dragon Isles

Liza

Cherry

Rena

Sasha

www.ingramcontent.com/pod-product-compliance
Lightning Source LLC
Chambersburg PA
CBHW031211020726
47499CB00002B/540